Whispered Voices

Storm Voices , Volume 1

Victoria LK Williams

Published by Sun, Sand & Stories Publishing, 2018.

This is a work of fiction. Similarities to real people, places, or events are entirely coincidental.

WHISPERED VOICES

First edition. January 1, 2018.

Copyright © 2018 Victoria LK Williams.

ISBN: 978-1393804154

Written by Victoria LK Williams.

For those who believe not everything has to have a logical answer...

Prologue

They say you can tell when a storm is coming, but only if you pay attention. Growing up along the Florida shoreline, I should have known this. When you grow up here, the signs are easy to see. It's second nature to watch for them.

When a storm is near, there are subtle changes. There may be a shift in the wind that brings the salty smell of the sea onshore, the temperature can fluctuate from ever so slight to drastic, and the seabirds' flight pattern could take a sudden turn. If you watch the clouds as they cover the horizon, you can see the storm approaching from miles away. The sky gets darker, the wind picks up, and the temperature drops. There's static to the air, even though there's no thunder or lightning. You can feel the change starting around you.

But only if you're paying attention. That day I let my guard down, and I wasn't paying attention. The storm come up on me without warning, and I paid the price.

That was the day everything changed, and my life suddenly went in directions I have never conceived.

The day I heard the first storm voice.

Chapter 1

It was hot. Hot as only August in Florida can be. But it wasn't only the weather that was hot, so was the topic of conversation. The one I was having with the hot guy sitting next to me on the beach. I'd been in love with him since high school, but he didn't know it; I settled for being his best friend. I suffered through the current conversation while he bemoaned the rockiness of his newest love affair.

But being the best friend that I am, I commiserated with him, trying to help him out as best as I could. He didn't have a clue about how I felt, and I would have been mortified if he ever found out. Somehow, I'm sure that little tidbit of news would ruin the most important friendship I had.

Peter and I have known each other most of our lives, but not until our high school years did we became fast friends. Our friendship began when I beat him in a cross-country race. After that, we started training and competing together, and through the sweat and tears, we formed a bond that lasted through the years. I'm always "Mac" to him. Not Mackenzie, my real name, which I think is much more regal and noteworthy, but just Mac. I don't know if he even noticed I've grown into an attractive woman since I was just his buddy, and that was enough for both of us. Until I left home to go away to college, that is. Only then did I realize how important he was to me. They say that absence makes the heart grow fonder, but my heart about broke with the emptiness of his absence. Oh, I tried dating. I even made some good friends, but none compared to Peter. I was thankful and relieved when, after six long years, I graduated and came back home to take my place in the family business.

But Peter had moved on, and he was dating a string of girls that made my head spin. I told myself that if he kept changing dates, it meant he wasn't getting serious about them, and I still stood a chance. Someday, I reasoned, by some miracle, he would wake up and see me for the woman I had become. Of course, it would take a miracle, because the fear of rocking the boat kept me from taking a stand and proclaiming my love for him.

So today we sat on the beach, in our favorite spot, and I listened to him complain about the failure of yet another date.

"I don't get it, Mac. I mean, this girl is gorgeous, smart, and looking for a long-term relationship. All the things a guy would want, but there was just no spark. It was like we were going through the motions. I took her to a movie, and we went to a nice restaurant, yet I knew halfway through the meal it wasn't going anywhere."

"Well, what movie did you go to? A nice romantic-"

"Of course not. We watched the newest Avenger movie. You would have loved it, Mac."

I laughed out loud. Sometimes Peter didn't have a clue. I mean, what girl wants to go to an action movie on their first date. Most girls would want a little romance, a little wooing. Myself included.

"Peter, you can't treat the girls you're dating like one of the guys. They want and deserve to feel special."

I tossed the sand I had been sifting through my fingers in his direction and he had the grace to look embarrassed. Shrugging his shoulders, Peter admitted that I was right. Putting his hands behind his head, he stretched out on the warm sand and sighed, closing his eyes. I think he knew he had blown it with this girl. I mentally gave a cheer. Deciding that he needed a little time to think, I got to my feet. Grabbing my straw hat, I turned and started walking down the beach, searching the sand for the elusive blues and greens of the sea-glass.

I passed two old fishermen, heading to the boardwalk and the beach's exit. We knew each other from years of sharing the same beach and exchanged a friendly hello. Now, it seemed I had the beach to myself. I guess no one else wanted to swelter in the ninety-degree heat, not when they could be cooling off inside, where there's air conditioning. The heat didn't bother me; I was used to it. A gentle breeze blew enough to dry the sweat off, and if it got too bad, I figured I could always jump into the ocean waves to cool myself off. The beach to myself, the sun and breeze and crashing waves of the Atlantic, was my idea of paradise.

I must have walked farther than I realized because when I looked around me next, I couldn't even see Peter. The wind had picked up and I put both hands on my head to keep my hat from blowing away.

I wasn't nervous about walking the sands on my own, but something made the hairs on the back of my neck stand at attention. There was still no one else at the strip of beach with me, but the air had changed. There was a static to it that tried to warn me, but I didn't notice the warning until it was too late. The static became supercharged and a flash of light like I'd never seen before in my life, blinded me. Everything suddenly went black.

Chapter 2

"**M**ac, oh Jesus, Mac, be okay."

I heard the pleading in Peter's voice, and I tried to reassure him I was fine, but the words wouldn't form. He said more, but the words were too far off to understand. Everything faded again.

The next thing I remember is opening my eyes and seeing the blurry vision of an angel. But I don't think that was right, because that would mean I was dead. I didn't feel dead. I had heard that when you die, you feel no more pain. That's what made me sure I wasn't dead, the pain in my head was excruciating. A moan escaped me, and the angel moved closer, but my vision blurred and faded to dark. When she spoke, her words were faint as if from a far distance. She told me I would be okay.

Time passed before I woke again, but I lost track of how much. This time my eyesight was clear, but my head still hurt. Making the mistake of trying to move to look around, the pain inside my head was fast and sharp. The pain started at the base of my neck and darted forward over the top of my head to settle over my eyebrows. It made any migraine I had ever suffered before pale in comparison. I moaned, and, in an instant, Peter stood at my side.

With a gentle stroke, he pushed the hair away from my face, and I saw tears in his eyes. I guess I was hurt more than I realized for him to be this upset, and I tried to smile and reassure him.

"Jeez, Mac, you scared me to death. It's good to see you awake. Just stay with me. I need to get the doctor, he'll want to see you now that you're awake." As he spoke, Peter leaned over and gave me a kiss on the forehead. It was a brotherly kiss, but that didn't matter because the kiss made my heart beat a little faster. Thank goodness, he was on his way out the door when the heart monitor hooked up my arm, increased its tempo, and threatened to give away my secret.

By the time he returned with the doctor and a nurse trailing behind, I had myself back under control, and my heart was beating at its normal pace. The doctor gave me a thorough exam concentrating on my vision and responses. As he moved towards my lower extremities, he asked his nurse for a swab, and I looked into the face of the nurse as she responded.

My angel. I recognized her voice. Not only did I know her voice, but there was a deeper recognition, almost a recognition of souls. I didn't understand what was happening, but I had a premonition that somehow, this woman would be important in my future.

The doctor touched my leg, and I drew my breath in with pain. I hadn't realized that my leg hurt, but he sure made me aware of it. Peter heard my deep inhale, and he moved to my side, holding my hand for comfort. I turned my head slightly toward him and asked what I needed to be answered.

"What happened, and why am I in the hospital?"

My question hung in the air, and there was a moment of silence. The doctor broke the silence and started a rhetoric of long unpronounceable words as he tried to describe my symptoms and the cause. He lost me after the first sentence. I tried to follow his conversation, but my mind seemed to be fuzzy and concentration was impossible. Or, maybe it was hard to concentrate because Peter continued to hold my hand.

With a satisfied smile, the doctor finished his diagnosis and looked at me as if I was a good child and had listened well. I almost expected a lollypop for good behavior. He put his pen back into his front pocket, put my chart back on the hook at the end of the bed, said a meaningless goodbye, and left me in the care of my angel.

She smiled and patted my free hand with reassurance.

"Well Mackenzie, I can tell from your expression that, as usual, the doctor talked too fast and too technical for anyone to understand. I apologize for him, he's always in such a hurry. He means well, but he forgets to take the time to talk to his patients. Let me explain in terms you might follow easier."

As she spoke, she reached behind me to fluff the pillow to support my neck and make me more comfortable and then handed me a cup of ice water. I sucked the water through the straw to ease my parched throat.

"Mackenzie, a bolt of lightning struck you. Not directly, but in a flash-over. What that means is lightning struck the ground close to you, and the charge jumped from the ground to your leg. That's why your leg hurts so bad. There are burns on your leg. They will heal, and you may even have a scar, but that too will fade. You're a very lucky girl, six inches closer, and the bolt of lightning would have struck you directly." She watched me for a moment as if making sure I understood her words and continued.

"Now, you will have headaches for a while, and you may find that your hearing may give you a bit of trouble, but this will all fade away. And in no time, you'll be back to normal."

I looked at her in astonishment, and then over to Peter for confirmation. With a nod of his head, he agreed with the nurse. I looked back at her in disbelief. I couldn't believe it, I had been struck by lightning. It didn't matter if it was a flash-over or a direct hit, I had let the one thing I'd been warned against my entire life happen.

Florida is notorious for lightning strikes. The storms come up so quickly, and people are often caught unaware. I couldn't believe I'd missed the signs that I have been taught to watch for all my life. The tears welled up and my remorse change to embarrassment.

"Now, don't go sitting there feeling sorry for yourself or reprimanding yourself. There was nothing you could have done to prevent it. It's just something that happened. Right now, we need to concentrate on getting you healthy and back to your normal routine. And the first step is to get some rest."

I looked up at the woman standing next to me, startled. It was almost as if she had read my mind. But that couldn't be. Of course not. It was something much more mundane. Like the fact she was a good nurse, had been through this situation before, and could anticipate what her patients were up against. She gave me a smile of understanding, and as she moved to pull the covers up closer to my chin, I noticed her name tag. Moira, an unusual name. Possibly Scottish? I wasn't sure, but it seemed to fit her. She reached for my arm to take my pulse, and it was like a second bolt of electricity shot through me. I looked at her, wondering if she felt it too. When she gave a slight smile, I knew she had experienced the same thing. There was a strong connection between the two of us, one I didn't understand and one I'm sure that went beyond modern medicine.

Peter had been standing on the other side, unaware of the exchange between Moira and myself. He kept looking at me as if to make sure I was okay. Finally, I returned his look and gave him a smile of reassurance.

"Peter, go home. I'm sure you have plenty of things to do without standing here at my bedside. I'm fine. The doctors and staff will take good care of me. I'll be home before you have a chance to miss me."

Moira nodded her head in agreement. "She's right, you know. All she'll do for a while is sleep. I'm sure if you're here, Mackenzie will worry about you. You can come back at visiting hours later. By then, Mackenzie should feel more like herself."

Peter looked between us. "Understood," he said as he bowed to us. Despite my pain, I chuckled. "I'll swing by your house, Mac, and pick up some clothes for you to wear home tomorrow."

As the door closed behind him, I sighed with relief. That was odd because I was always comfortable, almost complete when I was with Peter. But today, it was all too much for me, and I wanted to be left alone. Without even realizing it, my eyes closed, and as I began drifting off again, I sensed a change in the atmosphere. A static in the air almost like earlier in the day. I tensed in fear. The comforting touch of Moira, as she patted my hand, eased my tension, and I drifted off peacefully.

Chapter 3

I don't know what the doctor gave me, but it was strong. The next time I opened my eyes, the room was in darkness, and I was alone. I didn't bother to try and lift my head; I could vividly recall the pain from last time. Instead, I took in a visual summary of what I could see directly in front of me. The TV was on low, set to music. Funny, it wasn't music I usually would listen to, but it was soothing, and I enjoyed it. I could hear the beeping of the monitors as they recorded my every heartbeat. At least I knew I was still alive. I closed my eyes for a moment, and I swear that my senses were tingling in heightened awareness. I could smell things that I usually wouldn't have noticed, and I was more aware of the noises outside of the room than what should be possible with the music from the TV on.

I was also more aware of my own body, feeling each finger and toe acutely, and I swear I could feel the blood making its journey through them. It seemed odd to be so aware of myself.

I still had a headache, but it wasn't as bad as it had been. The pain in my ankle was now more of an irritant and I longed to reach down to rub it. This was a clear sign the medicine dripping into my IV was doing its job. Before I could contemplate the dilemma any further, the door cracked open and Peter stuck his head in.

"Hey, Mac, are you awake?" His whisper wasn't exactly soft, but he meant well.

"Yeah, come in, Peter." My voice cracked, and I realize my throat was dry. Peter must've heard the hoarseness in my voice because he reached over and poured me a glass of water and brought it to me as he walked into the room. He held the straw for me so that I could get a

10

good swallow, and then he set the cup back down after I assured him I had plenty for now.

"You have no idea how glad I am that you're okay, Mac. You gave me the biggest scare of my life. I really thought I'd lost you."

I could hear the sincerity of his emotions, and I tried to blink back the tears. Peter must've seen them because he reached over and gently wiped the corner of my eyes. Before either of us could say anything, the tender moment disappeared as a nurse came in. It wasn't Moira, and I felt disappointed. The woman quickly went about her business, taking my temperature, blood pressure, and then adjusted the bed so that I could sit up more comfortably. I was amazed that the headache from earlier had gone from a pounding to a dull ache. When she left, I pointed to the end of the bed.

"Peter, can you pull the blanket off? They said I would have a scar and I'd like to see how bad the burn is."

"I'm not taking the bandages off, so I don't know what you think you're going to see."

Before we could go any further, the door opened again, and this time it was Moira. She took in the situation in a glance, realized what Peter was doing with the blanket. Shaking her head, she chastised me for my impatience.

"This will not heal properly if you take the dressing off before it's ready. And you, sir, did you sterilize your hands before touching her?"

Peter dropped the blanket like a hot potato and blushed. I could see the smile lurking on the corners of Moira's mouth as she turned to me.

"You're not going to be at ease until you see this, are you? All right, I'll take the dressing off, and you can take a peek. And that's it—I'm going to get that wound covered right back up, so the medicine can do its job. Then, maybe you can stop worrying."

She worked with gentle hands that were skillful and efficient. I didn't even feel the pull of the dressing as she lifted it off, inch by inch. She then helped me to a more upright position and held me sturdy as I leaned over to look at my ankle. She was right, there was a scar there. It wasn't a cool scar like the one JK Rowling had given her character, Harry Potter, but it was interesting. It had the faint resemblance of a feather etched into my skin, and it seemed to circle my ankle, wandering a bit up my calf. If I'd been into tattoos, I probably would've wanted it to stay. But I had always taken pride in my legs, they were probably my best feature, and I was disappointed that they were now marred.

I hadn't realized that Peter was looking over my shoulder as well, and his voice made me jump. He grinned and gave me a thumb-up.

"On anybody else, that would be a scar. But on you, Mac, it's a beauty mark."

His words made me feel better, and I couldn't help but smile as I blushed. Any compliment from Peter was a gift. He just didn't give them out often, to me anyway. Satisfied that I had seen enough of my ankle, my caretaker eased me back onto my pillows and then deftly re-bandaged my injury. She then turned to both of us with a serious look on her face.

"Mackenzie, they will not allow you to stay here for long, beds are needed for other patients, as I'm sure you know. But you're going to need some care when you get home. That ankle is going to be sore to walk on, and your headaches are going to be intense for a while. We still need to monitor your hearing. You will need somebody to stay with you for the first couple of days, and then a therapist from the hospital will come daily to check on you. Do you have someone to stay with you?"

I knew I could call one of my girlfriends, and they would be there in a second to help me. But they would also hover and try to take over—I dreaded the thought. Before I could decide who would be the easiest to get along with for a couple of days, Peter chimed in.

"I'll stay with her," he stated in a somewhat bossy manner, clearly still concerned.

I was astonished. I knew we were best friends, but this was a lot for somebody to do.

"Peter, you don't have to do this. I have plenty of girlfriends nearby, and they can do this. Besides, you have a job to go to."

"You know as well as I do that I can work from home—it's one of the perks of working in my father's business, I can make my own hours. Besides, my parents would agree, taking care of the people you love always comes before work. Come on, Mac, you would do this for me."

He was right on all points, and I was thrilled that he had offered. Having my best friend with me when I needed him would be the best therapy I could get. I gave a nod to him and then turned to Moira.

"Okay, I guess I have a roommate for a couple days."

"Well, that's just perfect. Peter, I'll get you a list of supplies that she will need and directions for her care. The doctor told me she'll be released tomorrow afternoon, so you'll have time to get yourself set up." She looked pleased that everything was working out so well and then looked back at me, ready to give me my instructions as well.

"Right now, I would like you to get some more rest. In the morning, you'll have some testing done on your eyesight and hearing. You'll also need to be fitted for a crutch. Your friend can stay for fifteen minutes, and then I want you lying back down healing."

I gave her a thumbs-up, and Peter indicated that he understood her instructions as well. As soon as the door closed behind her, Peter sat on the edge of the bed and held my hand as we talked. Those fifteen minutes went by fast and before I knew it, Peter was saying goodnight, promising to be there tomorrow for my release. I made him promise not to come in the morning, worried that he would fall behind in his work.

Before he left, he gave me a light kiss on the forehead and then dimmed the lights as he walked out the door.

I laid back and close my eyes, content, and tired, and I snuggled into a more comfortable position. I was just about to doze off when I heard someone to the right of my bed. I felt too tired to open my eyes, assuming it was just another nurse. She didn't ask me any questions, but instead, I heard the woman's voice say the oddest thing.

"This is the one. There is immense potential here, powers waiting for instruction. But she will need guidance and wisdom to get her to accept them."

Chapter 4

When the orderly came to get me for all my testing the next morning, I still felt half asleep. It wasn't until Moira shone the light in my eyes to check my vision, that I remember the voice I had heard the night before. I pushed her hand away and asked what powers she found last night when she was in my room.

Moira looked at me with questioning eyes and then told me nobody had been in my room. She sounded positive, saying she checked herself to make sure I was undisturbed.

"Well, I know I heard somebody standing right next to me. And it wasn't just the words, the tone of her voice sounded pleased, almost in awe about something."

"I'm not sure who, or what you heard, but let's get to these tests right now and concentrate on one thing at a time."

I knew the tone of her voice, I had remembered it from all those times my mother had spoken with the same tone. It meant the conversation was over. Nothing I said would get her to finish answering my questions. And maybe Moira had a point, with all I had been through, it was probably my imagination working overtime.

She finished checking my eyes and then moved on to my hearing. I must admit I was relieved when she told me the tests were normal. The last thing I needed was to have problems with my hearing. Then it was down to physical therapy to get my crutch and be shown how to use it properly. By the time my therapy finished, I was ready to hit somebody with the crutch, but I kept my patience and allowed the orderly to wheel me back to my room, where I hoped to finally get some peace and quiet. But more nurses were waiting for me, and this time they wanted to change the dressings on my burn. Talk about painful. By the time they finished, I was ready to cry. I was sore, tired and wanted to go home.

Thankfully, that's when Peter walked in the door. The smile on his face lifted my spirits a little, but not as much as the doctor who walked in behind him with my release papers. I almost jumped out of my bed with excitement. The care I received had been excellent, but there was nothing like being in your own home and in your own bed. Plus, I had the bonus of Peter staying with me to look forward to.

The doctor ran through his instructions quickly. I shook my head, not even bothering to pay attention. Peter took diligent notes, taking his role of nursemaid seriously. After the doctor shook my hand and left the room with instructions for my follow-up visits, I felt as if a weight was off my shoulders. Moira came to the door after the doctor left, and with her came a sense of calmness and serenity, which put me at ease. She went over the doctor's instructions a bit slower, and in terms I understood, making sure I knew exactly what I could and couldn't do. She surprised me by giving me a hug before I left, and it seemed like I was leaving a family member behind.

Peter insisted on pushing the mandatory wheelchair down to his car, with the orderly following behind, warning him to slow down and be careful. But Peter was like a little kid wanting to see how far he could go before being reprimanded. This was a side of him I hadn't seen in a long time. By the time we reached the car, my head was spinning. He must've seen the exhaustion on my face and he quickly apologized, taking great care to make sure my seatbelt was buckled up and that I was comfortable. His hands lingered on the door before he closed it as he looked down at me, and I wondered what he was thinking.

The ride home passed in a blur. I must've slept part of the way because before I knew it, Peter gently shook my shoulder. He was on my side of the car, door open ready to help me into the house. I reached for the crutch, but he would have none of it and swept me in his arms and carried me to the front door. Any other time I would have felt like a princess, but I was just too tired, too sore, and too eager to get in bed and sleep.

Peter made sure to settle me comfortably in bed, tucking a blanket around me and putting a glass of water on the nightstand where I could easily reach it.

"Yell if you need anything, Mac," he said, before walking out of the door and closing it behind him. closing the door, he walked out

Before I knew it, it was morning. I guess I dozed on and off most of the night, never in a deep sleep, but getting the rest my body needed. I woke to hear the shower in the guest room running, and I thought longingly of being able to take one for myself. But I had to wait for the physical therapist to show up, to properly tape up my leg to be sure no water got on the wound or the dressings. Stretching my arms over to the nightstand, I grabbed my brush, deciding I would at least look presentable before I saw anyone.

I had just put my brush back when Peter knocked and popped his head into the room, his easy-going grin back in place. I had seen little of it yesterday, which told me how worried he had been.

"Good morning, Mac. You ready for some breakfast? Your home care nurse will be here in about half an hour. Need any help getting up and about?"

I waved off his offer of help. I could get to the bathroom on my own, thank God. Leaning against the sink for support, I brushed my teeth and washed my face. This would have to be good enough for now. Hopping my way to my closet, I grabbed a sun-dress, making sure to pick one of my short ones. Somehow, I was sure material touching my burn, no matter how soft, might be painful. By the time I zipped up the side of the dress, my breath was short from the excursion.

The knock at my bedroom door put an end to that wishful thought, and Peter stood there ready to help me out to the other room. He glanced around and shook his head when he noticed the crutch, still leaning against the wall where he had placed it the night before.

"Why didn't you use your crutch to get around? I heard you hopping around in here. To be honest, I was sure I would have to come in here and pick you up after you fell on your backside. You never do things the easy way, do you, Mac?"

I grunted a reply, not willing to tell him I hadn't even thought of using the crutch. Peter was right, I was stubborn, but not stupid. Sticking my tongue out as I took the crutch from him and started towards the living room.

The person sitting on my sofa could not have been more unexpected. Not that I knew what to expect, but it certainly hadn't been Moira. I broke into a huge smile. Although I had been eager to leave the hospital yesterday, I had also been sad to say goodbye to my Angel. Now she was here, and her presence filled the room with calm and peacefulness.

"Good morning, Mackenzie. You seem surprised I'm here. Didn't I promise we would see each other again?"

"Yes, you did. But I figured you were simply being polite, making small talk. I'm glad it's you, Moira, welcome to my home, such as it is."

"Well, I do outpatient work too, and I was ready for a new client. We seemed to have clicked, don't you think? That's so important for your recovery that you have a connection with your therapist. Now, first things first. Sit down and elevate your leg so it doesn't swell. I'll check the dressing and get new cream on the burn, then we'll talk. Peter, would you mind giving us some time alone?"

When I nodded okay, he walked over to the front door.

"If you two will be okay without me, I'd like to run over to my place and take care of a few things. Would an hour be enough time?"

"A perfect solution. Oh, would you mind bringing in the basket I left by the door, Peter? Be gentle with it." Moira gave him a smile as she made her request.

She was silent for a moment, and then with a delicate touch, she looked after my burn. "Your little jolt from mother nature has left you with an unusual mark. I'm afraid it will probably scar, but it is rather beautiful in its way. The feathering pattern winds around your ankle like a bracelet, and it's very intricate. Almost more like a painting rather than a scar."

I looked at Moira, wondering if she was serious. I could tell from the way she looked over the burn mark she was. Great. This wouldn't be a problem if I lived somewhere cold and wore heavy socks and boots. But I lived in Florida, and I lived in flip-flops. How could I hide a scar circling my entire ankle?

Moira seemed to read my thoughts, and she gave a slight shake of her head. "Why would you want to hide this, Mackenzie? Let me tell you a tale my grandmother told me about the fairies of the green, back in her home country."

I made a face and thought *if you must*, as she continued. I didn't want to listen to an old story about a country I'd never seen or planned to. But as she talked, my interest caught. I leaned forward, listening to her every word.

Chapter 5

"**M**y family has always held dear the stories that were passed on through the generations of those who lived in Scotland and those who came to America. As the years have passed, many have forgotten the stories or have dismissed them as untrue, just a poor man's way of passing the time. But my grandmother and her mother firmly believed the stories of the fairies and their mighty Queen, Shaylee. They were both in awe and afraid of them. So, listen closely as I tell you what was told to me when I was a young girl. You can dismiss what I say as a fairytale, or you can listen to your heart and come to your own conclusion."

As she spoke, Moira gently put the medication on my burn and the coolness eased the pain.

"I have always been told that fairies stay clear of humans. Yet, occasionally there will come a human who will grab their interest. The queen fairy, Shaylee, seems to be the one with the most interest in humans. For good or bad, she will decide if a human deserves her attention, and they will take their actions. Once the fairy has decided that you are worthy of their attention they will put their fairy mark on you. We humans call this a scar."

I looked down at my ankle, wondering if a fairy indeed decided I was worth noticing. I wasn't sure if that was a good thing or a bad thing, but something told me Moira's story would help me decide. I continued to listen to her, noticing that the more she spoke, the more pronounced her Scottish accent became.

"Now sometimes you might be but a babe, and the scar will appear during your birth. It is said the scar is for some good deed that your parents did before the birth. A small little scar or birthmark was like a fairy blessing, and there's nothing we can do about a baby's fairy mark." Moira paused in her story, and her voice lowered as if she was deep in thought. "Maybe someday I will tell you about the types of scars and birthmarks I've seen on the many newborns I've cared for over the years."

"My grandmother used to tell me that when you got a scar in your later years, it was often because you did something foolish and the fairy's protected you. Your scar was a fairy kiss. Your special fairy left the scar there to remind you of your mistake, so you wouldn't repeat it. The scar like yours, Mackenzie, a scar that was by accident, has a special meaning. Your scar looks like a piece of artwork, so it is a true fairy kiss. Because of the circumstances and the size of your scar, my grandmother would say the fairies have touched you for a special purpose."

I looked at Moira like she had lost her mind. Even if I believed in fairies, why would they select me as someone special? There are no heroic acts in my past. I've never rescued somebody or done something clever and thought-provoking to change the way things went on in the world around me. No, I was just me. I get along with people, I care about people, and I stand up for people's rights when I suspected they were being trampled on by a bully. But, so did most of my friends. It wasn't anything special.

"Ah, I see you doubt my story. Time will tell, Mackenzie, if you will believe me or not. Often, a fairy kiss brings with it unusual abilities you didn't have before. It might be something as simple as being more in tune with the surrounding people, being more aware of their feelings or needs. Then again, it might be something else. It might even take a while for you to find out what it is. When you do, we'll discuss more of this tale and whether your new abilities are real or not."

Moira's storytelling ability kept me so engrossed in listening to her tale, that I never noticed she had finished with my ankle. Giving me a pat on the knee, she told me to sit still for a few minutes and then she would have me get up and walk. I closed my eyes for a moment, picturing the queen fairy, Shaylee, fluttering in the room, giving anybody in sight a fairy kiss. With my eyes closed, I didn't notice Moira get up and walk away, but a few seconds later I heard her singing in the kitchen and the running of tap-water reached me. I snuggled into the soft cushions of the couch, enjoying my few moments alone with my silly thoughts.

"He's mine, you can't have him."

I sat upright at the words and looked around me. I knew I heard the words, but I saw no one. I couldn't even see Moira from this position. I rubbed my ears vigorously, wondering if I was hearing things. But in my heart, I didn't think so. The voice was clear and sounded so full of passion, and anger. But how could I explain it to someone else? Deciding to keep it to myself, I waited for Moira to return from the kitchen. No, I would definitely not be telling anybody I was hearing voices. Hopefully, it was just an after-effect from the lightning strike and it would go away. Maybe it was a remnant of a dream that wouldn't leave my mind.

The front door opened as Peter returned. He was whistling with an easy smile for Moira as she walked out from the kitchen. All seemed right in his world, and I knew that smile. He had connected with a girl again, and I wondered if it was the same one from his botched date.

When Moira saw him, she took him by the arm and led him into the living room to sit with me.

"Good, I'm glad you're back, Peter. I have a few simple instructions for the two of you. My job is done for now, and I will be back tomorrow again at about the same time."

Moira stopped me before I could speak, back in full nurse duty, the storyteller persona put away for the time being. She gave us strict instructions about me walking around a little bit and then elevating my leg. Peter assured her he would take diligent care of me. I was surprised at the passion in his voice.

"Oh, Peter, can you hand me my bag?"

Peter picked up the bag and almost dropped it in the same motion. His eyebrows rose when the bag shifted in his hands under its own power. Walking over to Moira, he gingerly held the bag out to her. She smiled at his reaction, pulled the bag open, and reached inside to pull out a small gray kitten with the bluest eyes I've ever seen.

"I took it upon myself to bring this poor little lost kitten to you. I found it last night. I knocked on a few doors to see if anybody had lost it, but the poor baby is unclaimed and alone. Can you find it in your heart, Mackenzie, to look after this poor little thing? She's sure to be good company for you. I even stopped and got everything she would need, and she'd already shown me she knows how to use a litter box. What do you say, can you take this poor little thing under your wing?"

The kitten gazed at me with her big blue eyes. How could I possibly say no? The kitten just oozed cuteness, and when I reached out for it, she snuggled comfortably in my arms.

"Well Moira, there's your answer," laughed Peter.

In three seconds that little kitten endeared itself to me and as I scratched behind her ears, hearing her purr, nothing could convince me to give her back. Moira gave a nod of satisfaction. She had found a place for the orphan and had given me something to concentrate on other than myself. It was a perfect solution.

Peter smiled as he reached out to scratch her chin. "What are you going to call her, Mac?"

I didn't even hesitate. "Shaylee," I said as I gave Moira a teasing grin.

Chapter 6

After Moira left, I had a quiet evening playing with the kitten and talking to Peter. It felt like old times, the two of us spending a friendly evening together, catching up on the day's news. I didn't last very long, and it was another early night for me.

I woke the next morning to find Peter taking on his role of being responsible for my wellbeing, as he insisted that I settle down while he fixed breakfast. Granted, it wasn't much of a breakfast, an overly toasted piece of bread with peanut butter slapped on it, but he meant well.

"I hope this is good enough for you, Mac. You know I'm not very good in the cooking department. But at least your tea is strong," smiling ruefully, he placed it in front of me.

When I was done, Shaylee jumped up on my lap, circled three times and settled down as if to say 'nap-time.' I found myself exhausted by the effort of sitting up to eat, so I agreed with her sentiment. Curling up next to Shaylee, I fell fast asleep. I didn't even wake up when Peter came in and placed a blanket over me.

The next thing I knew, I woke up to find the kitten had moved from my lap to my shoulder and was curled up against my neck, purring softly. I saw Peter sitting across from me, working on his laptop. Sensing I was awake, he closed his laptop and came over and gently brushed the hair out of my eyes.

"Hey, Mac. Feeling any better? Your color's back, and you look more like your old self."

I gave Peter a smile, and he helped me back up to a sitting position. I enjoyed being pampered by Peter. He had always treated me as an equal, or even like one of the guys, and I secretly hoped that my unexpected weakness would make him think of me differently. It would be nice if he noticed me as a woman rather than his best friend, I thought for the umpteenth time.

"How about if we put that kitten down for a little bit, and you take your first walk? Anyplace in particular you want to go?"

I didn't need to even think about an answer, my body told me exactly where I needed to go, and I pointed towards the bathroom. Peter grinned, and true to his promise to Moira, he kept his hand on my back, supporting me to make sure I didn't fall to and from the bathroom.

"Peter, you don't have to babysit me," I said after I got settled back on the couch. "Honest. If there's something else that you need to do, go ahead and do it."

Peter chuckled and pulled something out of his back pocket. "I believe I owe you some money. How about giving me a chance to win it back? You think you're up for a game of poker?"

I laughed out loud and grabbed the pack of playing cards from his hands. He never learned, and although I never collected on the money he owed me, I never let him win the game either. Peter's downfall was he never mastered the skill of bluffing. Or maybe it was because I knew him so well, and I could read the subtle changes in his expressions.

"You're on, Peter."

We played until Moira arrived, with Peter losing miserably as usual. She dismissed Peter as she had the day before and settled down to change my dressings. With her business completed, Moira told me more stories from her ancestral home in Scotland. At times, I thought for sure she was teasing me, and at other times she peered at me with a curious expression. I found her to be a fascinating woman, and it surprised me that we had so much in common.

The rest of the week passed in much the same way. The only difference was that Moira stayed longer, spending time with me as a friend, rather than a nurse. As I regained the strength in my leg, Peter returned to his normal routine. He still insisted on staying with me at night, and I didn't fight him. By the end of the week, I had the feeling that he had started seeing someone, just by his demeanor and his beaming face.

"Are you giving that poor girl you took to the movies a second chance?"

"No, you're right, I blew that one. Someone I dated a long time ago is back in town and wanted to get together. I'm not sure if you ever met her or not. Isabella?"

"That name sounds familiar, so maybe you introduced us, or you talked a lot about her. Are you getting serious?" I asked, holding my breath, afraid to hear his answer.

"I can't tell. She's fun to be with, and I think she wants to get serious, but there's something missing. We'll see what time brings."

I let out a discrete sigh of relief. If he was holding back on this relationship, then I figured it wouldn't work out. Peter is an all-or-nothing type of guy.

Since I work from home, I decided on Saturday morning that I could hobble to my home office. I worked as a charity coordinator for a few of the local charities; my pay a pittance. That didn't matter, at least not to me. I came from a wealthy family and the funds were at my disposal to use as I wished. Peter was aware of my situation, having grown up with me, but even he wasn't aware of how well off I was. When my parents died, they left me a wealthy orphan. So, it became my responsibility, and my lawyers, to disperse the money my family left behind to make sure it went to beneficial use. I'm not a frivolous person, and I didn't need much for myself. I think the most I ever indulged in were ball gowns for the charity events I was obligated to attend. Even those purchases were from my favorite consignment shop.

My lawyer is also my godfather, my father's best friend. Uncle Charlie had always been there to look out for me. He approved of my decision to work for the charity organization and agreed keeping quiet about my wealth seemed the smartest thing I could do. Uncle Charlie had already visited me a few times since my injury and, once he was assured I was getting the best care possible, and he met Moira, he seemed relieved. The two of them hit it off, just as Moira and I had.

"She's a smart one, that Moira. Smart in many ways, and she seems to have your goodwill at heart. Friends like that are scarce, Mac. So, treasure this one."

I acknowledged his words as true; I realized just how lucky I was that Moira had come into my life.

On Monday evening, I convinced Peter and Moira to stay and taste a new recipe I found on the Internet. The three of us finished dinner, and they deemed it a success, eating more than their fair share. Myself included. Moira volunteered to do the dinner dishes, and Peter made his way to my office to work on a computer problem I had developed that day. That left me with Shaylee, purring with contentment while curled up on my lap, to catch the evening news.

About five minutes into the evening newscast, Peter's cell phone rang. Glancing around, I realized that he had left it sitting on the coffee table in front of me. He heard it from my office and told me to answer it for him. Picking it up, I saw it was the phone he only used for communicating with his family since his grandmother had been so ill over the last year. Thinking there might be an emergency, I hurriedly answered. My voice seemed to startle whoever was on the other line, and silence greeted me for a moment—then the person spoke. I knew the voice, I knew the tone, I knew the anger, and I knew what words were coming before the words even came, sending chills up and down my spine.

"He's mine, you can't have him."

I dropped the phone like a hot potato. How could it be? How could the killer have Peter's private number, I knew he never gave it to anyone. Yet it was the same female voice, saying the same words I'd heard a few days ago. Whoever was on that line knew me and was making her claim on Peter. I looked down at the screen only to find there was no number for a callback.

The burning sensation in my ankle brought me back to reality. I looked down at my ankle in astonishment. There hadn't been any pain in a couple of days, but the pain scorched as if fresh, and I reached down to rub it. Shaylee snapped to attention, and when my hand moved closer to my ankle, she reached out and slapped it. I looked at her astonished, and with her blue eyes wide, she gave one little shake of her head as if telling me no.

"Hey, Mac, who was on the phone?" Peter yelled out.

Looking down at the phone on the floor made me wonder if I'd lost my mind. I must be overly tired, and my imagination was working overtime. "It was only a wrong number," I responded, trying to convince myself. I glanced over to Shaylee as if she might have an answer for me, and I noticed her gazing off towards the kitchen. I turned my head to find Moira standing at the kitchen counter, watching me.

Chapter 7

It wasn't long after the three of us had settled down in the living room, me with my leg elevated again, that we were ready to play a game of poker. Peter was determined to win, and Moira had asked to be taught the game. I had a feeling that once she mastered it, she would be a ferocious opponent, and Peter would be sorry. What I really wanted to do was to speak to Moira alone, but she had received a call and had to leave for the hospital. I sensed she wanted to talk to me too, but Peter was underfoot all night. Not that I minded, of course. But somehow, I felt that my new friend held answers for me, and when the time was right, she would explain things. I'm not sure I wanted any explanations from her, I feared what her tales of Fairy's would weave through them. I wasn't sure how seriously she took the stories she told; was she entertaining me, or did they have a hold on her?

Once Peter and I were alone, we were no longer in the mood to play a card game.

"How's the ankle feeling, Mac? Do you think you'll be up and moving around like normal soon?"

"It's doing much better. I can tell when I've overdone it, and I get random twitches and shots of pain, but mostly it's just a matter of keeping the swelling down. Moira's positive I'll be up and moving around by the end of the week on my own. I hope the scar fades, because, as you know, I'm not one for wearing shoes and socks and I'm not going to start, merely to hide it."

Peter reached over and traced the scar with his fingertip, sending all kinds of wonderful feelings racing through my body. When Shaylee jumped up and slapped his hand away, the look of astonishment on his face made me burst out laughing.

"What's with her? Anyways, why would you want to hide it? It's like a war wound, only on you it looks pretty."

I ignored the compliment as I picked up the cat and looked at her straight in the eyes, scolding her for slapping at Peter.

"I don't know what's with Shaylee. She slapped me today too when I touched my ankle. You may think the scar is pretty, but it is a scar, and as vain as it sounds, I'm not at all happy about having one."

The cat butted her head against mine, almost as if she was rebuking me. I scratched her behind the ears and put her back down the floor, where she walked away, with her tail in the air.

"I wouldn't worry about the scar, Mac. You've always had the best set of legs in the group."

"Gee, thanks. Considering the group you're talking about consists mostly of guys, I would call that a pretty backhanded compliment," I laughed.

Peter blushed. "I'm sorry."

"No worries, Peter. I knew what you meant. Anyways that movie you wanted to watch is on tonight, so are we on?"

Peter answered by plopping down on the chair next to me and grabbing the remote, turning on the TV. When Peter's phone rang, the hairs on my neck stood up as he looked at the screen. He took me by surprise when he let out a moan of frustration and rejected the call. He saw my inquiring look and shrugged.

"Nothing important. I made tentative plans to meet someone over at Ollie's to listen to a new band, but I'd rather be here."

"Peter, if the guys are waiting for you, then go. We can do this another time."

He tugged on his ear, a habit he had when he felt embarrassed or uncomfortable. "Actually, it's not the guys. It's someone I used to date. I can't get through to her that I'm not interested in a relationship right now that goes beyond friendship. She's nice and all that, but we don't mesh all that well."

As he reached over to grab the bowl of popcorn, he gave me a brotherly hug as he teased. "Not the way you and I mesh, Mac."

I grinned back at him, thankful for the compliment. I was perfectly aware that he meant that in a friendship way, not romantically, but I'd take what I could get.

His phone buzzed again. This time the hairs on my neck did more than stand up, they tingled. I protested when he turned his phone off, not wanting him to miss going out on my account.

"Peter, have you told her how you feel?"

"Yeah, a couple of times. But it's not getting through to her. So, I guess I must be more direct and stop ignoring her. Come on, stop worrying-the movie's back on."

Within seconds, his attention was drawn back into the action on the screen, but I had a tough time dismissing the calls so easily. The movie was almost finished when a loud clap of thunder rattled the window panes, and lightning flashed across the sky.

"I won't be ignored, Peter. You'll notice me and forget all about her!"

The words were as clear as the thunder, and my ankle burned sharply. The anger and hate in the voice was apparent, and I looked over at Peter in a panic. But it was clear he hadn't heard a thing, and I wondered if I was losing my sanity.

As if sensing my distress, Shaylee jumped up on my lap and bumped her head against my chest. As I petted her, my tension slowly eased. But not the memory of that voice.

Chapter 8

A s the credits for the movie played, the meaning of the words of the voice sank in, and I stifled my gasp. I think somebody made a threat against Peter, and that deserved my full attention.

I decided that to find out what was going on, I needed to do two things: talk to Moira, and get information from Peter about this woman.

"Hey Peter, that girl you're talking about, have I met her?"

"I'm not sure if you have or not, Mac," he said, his eyes furrowed. "But, I wouldn't mind hearing what your opinion is of her, maybe you'd want to meet her? If we can get Moira to clear it, why don't we plan on going to Ollie's in the next couple of nights, and I'll set it up?"

Now I was in for it. I committed myself by showing my curiosity. But I felt it was necessary, for my own sanity, to prove I really had heard that voice. I was growing concerned about Peter's safety. He's a tall, somewhat muscular guy, but so was the lead character in *Fatal Attraction*.

"That's a great idea. I need to get out of the house, and Ollie's a wonderful place for my first time out. I'll talk to Moira about it in the morning."

"You two hit it off so well, why don't you ask her to join us? I think she'd enjoy the group playing this week."

Stretching his arms high above his head, Peter yawned, and I figured he was getting ready to leave. I grabbed the cane that I now used for support and walked to the door. With a brotherly kiss on the cheek, Peter said good night and promised to call me in the morning.

After I locked up behind Peter, I made my way to my bedroom. Although I went through the motions of getting myself ready for bed, sleep was far from coming. Walking over to the balcony, I opened the French doors, breathing in the sweet scent of Jasmine and wet rain. It was cooler now, thanks to the rain, and the moon hung high in the sky; the night was gorgeous. Since I was still wide awake, I grabbed a towel and wiped off the dew from one of the chairs before sitting down to enjoy the stillness of the evening. Shaylee followed me out and walked the perimeter of the balcony like a night watchman. Thoughts ran through my head, the most prevalent one had me wondering if I was losing my mind.

Tonight was the second time I had heard that same voice in my head. No one else seemed to hear it, although I wondered about the cat. Each time it happened, she seemed to be right there, her intelligent eyes looking at me as if she realized exactly what had happened. I was certain she had the answers, and I wish she could share them with me.

It didn't take long for the night sounds to calm my nerves, and I felt myself relaxing. Tomorrow I would talk to Moira. I figured if she didn't have the answers, she would at least have some common-sense directions.

The next morning was hot and humid, as only south Florida can be in the summer. All hints of the cool evening disappeared, and the sun had already evaporated the dew off the lawns. It should be a beach day, but that was out of the question for me. I wouldn't even waste the energy asking Moira if the doctor would release me to hit the sand. I would be better off pleading my case for an evening out to Ollie's. Besides, a pile of paperwork waited for me on my desk, needing my attention before this morning was over. The grant proposal's deadline was in a few days, and a lot of families relied on the funds from the grant.

I would have gladly given my own money to those who needed it so badly, but my lawyers put tight reins on how the family's fortune should be spent. I could use my personal money to raise funds, but not to give it away. As a result, much of my time entailed looking for ways to generate money through grants and fundraisers to help those in need. I spent most of my efforts on helping the farming families that migrated with the crop harvest. For many, there was no way to educate their children consistently because of the way they moved around, and healthcare also presented a huge issue for these families.

Pulling a lightweight sleeveless dress over my head, I got ready to start my day. I grabbed a hair tie out of a drawer and pulled my hair up into a messy bun. Teeth brushed, face moisturized, and lipstick applied; I headed to my office. Without realizing it, I walked across the room without the cane. My ankle didn't even twinge. By following Moira's instructions, I was healing fast. The ointments applied to the burn would not be needed much longer at this rate.

I made a side trip to the kitchen, but before I set the coffeemaker up, someone knocked at the back door. Moira pushed the door open as she called out, with two to-go cups, one of coffee and one of tea, in her hands. "I hope you don't mind my company so early. I was on my way to the hospital for my rounds and I had an unexplainable feeling that you needed to talk with me. So, I stopped and picked up our favorite drinks and here I am."

"Oh, Moira, that smells wonderful. Come on in. I don't know how you knew, but yes, I need to talk to you. How much time do you have?" As she walked towards the kitchen table, I grabbed a coffee from her and breathed in the wonderful aroma; coffee and hazelnut, what could start the day any better?

We sat in comfortable silence for a few minutes, enjoying our hot drinks. I told her about going to Ollie's and she said she'd think about it. Then, Moira waited for me to say something. I wanted to phrase my words just right; I didn't want to come off sounding like I'd lost my mind. The last thing I needed was for her to think I needed to be admitted back into the hospital-this time in the mental health ward.

Chapter 9

"That first day in the hospital, you told me I might suffer after-effects from the lightning strike. Didn't you say my hearing might also give me some problems?"

Moira sat up a little straighter in her chair, her eyes watching me with the same intenseness I often saw from Shaylee.

"Well, is it possible the shock to my system could make me hear things?" I asked, after her nod to go on. "The doctor said I might suffer some hearing loss, but is it possible to go the other way and, say, heighten my hearing?"

"One of the most common side effects is a loss of hearing and intense headaches. Are you experiencing either of those, Mackenzie?"

I loved that she didn't shorten my name the way everyone else did. And when she said my name, I caught a trace of her Scottish heritage. I assured her I was having neither of the two symptoms.

Hearing loss? I wish, I thought to myself before I answered.

Then I dropped my bombshell. "No, I'm not experiencing hearing loss, I think it's the opposite of that. Is it possible I can hear voices? They're random, and I hear them at the oddest times with no warning. Moira, they're so real I can hear the raw emotions from the speaker. I think Shaylee hears them too. But no one else. Peter was sitting not ten inches away from me and he didn't hear a thing. Do you think the lightning caused brain damage?"

There, I'd said it. The fear that had been haunting me since I left the hospital. I was suffering from brain trauma. It had to be, it was the only answer that made sense.

"That's the last thing you need to worry about, Mackenzie. There's nothing wrong with your mental abilities. I could give you a scientific theory for what you're going through, or there is another explanation. One that takes a big leap of faith on your part to believe this. Personally, I've felt since meeting you there is something special about your aura. You've been fairy-kissed, Mackenzie. And it has left you with a special ability. An ability which may take a bit to understand and get used to. Shaylee knows it too. She comes from a line of felines that once walked the glens where the fairies ruled. I found her former owner and could trace her lineage. This is why you sense Shaylee can also hear the voices. Because she can. She is here to help you stay calm when you hear one, to recognize the signs leading to an occurrence and keep you centered."

I almost snorted out loud. Yet, when I looked at Moira, I saw she was perfectly serious. Also, she had me believing her words. Heck, I was willing to believe almost anything she told me if it could explain what was going on.

"Do you mean to tell me you still believe in fairies? I mean, honestly, I've been convincing myself I'm not crazy. Then you come in with this completely off the wall theory. I'm not sure which option is worse."

"You asked my opinion, Mackenzie. I think you've been leading yourself down a pathway of doubt. You're just as convinced as I am, there is nothing mentally wrong with you. So, why can't you accept the other option I offer? Many things in our lives are unexplained. You've been given an unusual gift, even if it doesn't seem like it now. Wouldn't it be better to accept my theory and let me help you work through it?"

I gave her a thoughtful look, contemplating on what she said. I wanted to believe her, and her concept did intrigue me.

Shaylee jumped on the table and gently butted her head against mine, causing Moira to laugh. "See, even Shaylee's trying to tell you to follow your instincts and trust me."

"Okay, let's say you're right, and I've been 'fairy-kissed.' What does it mean, and why do I hear voices? How can you help? What do you really know about this?"

Moira took a sip of her tea before she answered. She set her cup down and reached across the table, taking my hands in hers. Her touch was comforting, and I felt myself relaxing. When she finally spoke, her voice was just as calm and reassuring as her touch.

"You're right, Mackenzie, in today's fast-paced age of modern technology, it's hard to imagine any of the stories from my childhood could possibly be true. But I know first-hand they are. My whole family has been fairy-kissed from the times of the earliest Clansmen. And it is our duty, because of this gift, to help others soothe their physical ailments and understand their own powers as they are given to them."

Moira pulled the sleeve of her shirt up for me to see a small birthmark on the inside of her elbow. I wasn't sure if she was trying to prove her point of bond with me.

"You're not the first one I have helped in my lifetime. But your powers are the strongest I've ever come across. I think the first thing to do, is you need to tell me, in detail, everything you can remember about the voice; when you heard it and any other circumstances that might have surrounded each instance. Once we know those details, it will be easier to figure out how to go forward and how to use your abilities. We need to train you to recognize the gift that is now part of you."

I stared at her, baffled. In my heart, I didn't question a word she said, and I trusted her. My logical mind might question the logistics and truth of this tale, but right now, I wanted to listen to what she had to say.

For the next half hour, I told her about the voices and told her that each time I heard the voice, Peter was nearby. Her head nodded with understanding as Moira had exceptional listening skills, without me coming across as a complete fool. She asked intelligent questions. Questions that made me think beyond the simple answer I was giving. Before I knew it, we were coming up with a theory.

"Something to consider Mackenzie. Both times the voice spoke, you were in extreme stress, or the surrounding air was full of stress and static from a storm. The first time, you were in the hospital, confused and afraid. Maybe that's why you heard the voice so clearly, because your senses were fully open."

"And last night? I couldn't have been more relaxed."

"Yes, you were relaxed, but the surrounding atmosphere was charged. Between thunder and lightning and the rain, it was a perfect setting. And in your relaxed state, you could hear the voices clearly."

"Well then, the easy thing to do is just to make sure I wear earplugs when there's a storm," I answered flippantly.

She smiled at my attempt at humor. "You're sure it was the same voice both times?"

"Oh yeah, it was the same voice. I will not forget that voice, or the tone, for a long time." I shuddered from the memory.

"Are you sure the voice was talking about Peter?"

I didn't hesitate to answer. I nodded my head vigorously, I was sure Peter was being threatened by the voice. Just thinking about it made the hair on the back of my neck bristle.

Moira nodded her head as if she had decided. She reached over and grabbed the empty cups and disposed them in the garbage can. She glanced down at her watch.

"Peter's right, you're ready for an evening out. I would enjoy going to Ollie's, too. It's important we both meet this woman he's talking about. We need to clarify if she is the voice you're hearing and what her intentions are."

She gave me a reassuring hug before she left. Shaylee took over the role of comforter, rubbing her head against my chin and then curling up on my lap. As I contemplated our conversation, I absent-mindedly stroked Shaylee's head and the sound of her purring filled the room.

Chapter 10

I looked forward to the night out at Ollie's with a mix of nerves and excitement. I was thrilled to be getting out of the house for an evening of fun. My nerves about meeting Peter's friend ran high, too. Could it be her voice I was hearing? Or worse, what if she was a perfect match for Peter? Moira and I arranged to meet Peter at Ollie's after she finished her rounds at the hospital. But that left me with the entire day to myself. For once, I had cleared my desk of work. I found myself at a standstill, waiting on responses from others about the fundraisers proposed for the upcoming season. No appointments were penned in on my calendar today, an unusual development. I'm good about keeping the housework caught up, so not even a cleaning project sat on the sidelines.

Shaylee followed me around as I wandered from room to room. When I ended up back in my bedroom, I decided to pick out something to wear for later. Even though I had hours to wait, I wanted to look my best. I didn't know anything about the woman I would meet, but to me, she was my competition. And when you meet your competition, you wanted to be at the top of your game.

I wanted something that would cover my new scar, but not tight or constricting. Thank goodness long summer dresses were back in style. I reached for a pale green summer dress. Pulling it out, I held it up against my body, noticing for the first time the shimmery purple undertone. Shaylee meowed her approval.

"This one, huh? It has an appeal, like something mystical. Maybe I'll grow fairy wings too." I giggled and swore the cat hissed a warning. I guess she didn't like my flippant attitude.

I decided that since my clothes were picked out, and there was nothing else to do, I'd go for a short walk along the beach. It had been too many days since my last visit, and I felt myself having withdrawal symptoms. If I took my time and rested before I walked back, I should be fine. I grabbed one of my favorite straw hats and slipped my feet into a more subdued pair of flip-flops than what I planned on wearing tonight. A quick swipe of lipstick and a smear of sunblock, and I was ready to go. As I picked up my phone and keys, a soft pressure against my injured leg caused me to peer down at Shaylee. Her gaze unblinking, as if she was trying to convey some message to me.

"I won't be gone long," I called out to Shaylee as I patted her head on the way out. "You go find a sunny spot and take a nap. We can sit out on the porch when I get back." I swear she knew exactly what I said, and her head nodded in agreement.

My garden was one of my favorite spots; walled away from the neighborhood, I had created a garden that rivaled the legendary Secret Garden of fiction, only planted full of tropical flowers. The wind teased the hat on my head, threatening to steal it away, and the taste of the salt in the air teased my taste buds. Already the sun felt hot; another scorcher was in store for those who dared stay on the beach longer than a few hours. There were few out to share the Boardwalk with me, other than a group of arguing seagulls and a lone pelican sitting on the railing. I had heard the waves were breaking perfectly for surfing farther up the coast. That's where most of our friends would be if they weren't working. It was the last days of summer break for students to enjoy before heading back for the next semester.

I felt myself being energized from the sun, and I closed my eyes and tilted my head back to absorb as much of the energy as possible from the beams of light and heat. I couldn't believe how good it felt to be back on the Boardwalk. With my eyes closed, I took in each and every detail: the sound of the surf against the beach, the cry of the seagulls, and the brush of the sea breeze against my skin.

I heard a deep voice calling my name. My eyes popped open and I blinked rapidly against the glare of the sun. I looked around and a grin broke out when I recognized my godfather. When he reached my side, he engulfed me in a huge bear hug, with a quick kiss on the cheek.

"Good morning. How did you find me, Uncle Charlie?"

"I figured I would find you here when I went to the house and no one answered. It's good to find you up and moving around, my girl. And since you are up and moving around, I'm assuming your leg is feeling much better?"

"Yes, Uncle Charlie, everything's healing up great." I hugged him back. We walked together for a bit until we came to one of the wooden benches scattered along the Boardwalk and we both sat down, admiring the beautiful sight in front of us. Out past the breaking waves, on the horizon, we saw large cargo ships, and we silently watched their progress.

"Well, that's enough outdoors for me today, it's getting hot and I'm in a suit. Can I interest you in a cup of coffee?"

I laughed. "Yes, I did notice you weren't wearing attire appropriate for the beach."

"Yep," he said as he stood up, arching his back to stretch it, "gotta go serve the masses."

I took the arm he held out, and we walked down the Boardwalk to our favorite coffee shop.

When we entered, calls of greeting rang out. My godfather was a popular lawyer around town, and I've lived here all my life, so to me, most of the people who lived here were family. He led me to a chair, always solicitous and looking out for me as if I was still the little girl he loved to take out for an afternoon treat. Then he moved forward to stand in line to place our order. The shop seemed relatively quiet, and his order was filled without delay; in a matter of minutes, he joined me at the table. I expected there might be more than coffee on the tray, and he didn't disappoint me. Uncle Charlie managed to secure two cherry

Danishes along with the coffee. He grinned as he placed the plate in front of me.

"Now, this is a good breakfast." He laughed as he took his first bite.

I grinned back at him, nodding my head in agreement. I loved spending mornings like this with my godfather. He could be serious and solemn, but then he was also fun-loving and full of mischief. You just never knew what mood you'd find him in.

We spent the next half hour talking and enjoying each other's company. The sound of his phone crooning out an old Patsy Cline song broke up our conversation and, looking at his watch, he apologized, saying he needed to take the call and get moving down to the courthouse. He gave me a quick kiss on the cheek and bid me goodbye, answering his phone as he walked out the door. As the door closed behind him, I looked down at my plate and realized half the Danish sat on the plate, waiting for me to finish. With no reason to hurry, I settled back to watch the comings and goings of the others in the coffee shop while I finished my treat.

By the time I finished eating, and talked to a few other patrons, I found that half a day had passed by already. I got to my feet, a little stiff and sore, and decided to head home.

Once home, I ended up in the old-fashioned wicker swing under the huge oak tree that covered most of the garden. With a book in hand, and Shaylee following me out, I intended to relax for the next few hours. I ended up being out there for longer than a few hours, and I woke up with my stomach rumbling and Shaylee gazing at me. After preparing Shaylee's dinner, I hurried to get myself ready for the evening out. Before I knew it, Moira had arrived to pick me up. I was anxious about tonight and wanted to have the opportunity to check out Peter's date before we met her. Yes, part of that was because of the voices I'd been hearing, but I had to be honest—the other part was because I wanted to size up my competition. Until a ring sat on Peter's finger, I would fight for him, even if I fought quietly in the background like a little mouse.

We timed it so that Ollie's was already busy. One band had already played their first set, loosening up the audience for the main act. The drinks were flowing, but since the evening had just started, the patrons were well behaved.

I led the way towards our usual table, greeting those that I knew. Moira kept close, and she acknowledged the introductions as I made them. I saw our usual table, and Peter and his date were already there. I felt myself tensing as I took in her appearance. She hadn't seen me yet, so I took in all I could about her. She appeared to be tall, curvy in all the right places with long, straight black hair. The noise level made it too hard to hear, but I saw her laughing at something Peter had said. Her head was thrown back and I saw her perfect teeth, and grinding my own, I watched her lean forward to flirt with Peter.

Peter looked over her shoulder and caught sight of us. His genuine smile warmed my heart, and it looked like he was glad we had arrived. Giving a wave, he motioned for us to join them. *Now is the moment of truth*, I thought to myself. I looked over at Moira, suddenly nervous. She squeezed my hand for comfort and encouragement. I took a deep breath and pasted a fake smile on my face, preparing myself to meet the dark beauty sitting at Peter's side.

"Hi, Moira. I'm glad you made it. Mac, you look great." Peter stood and kissed us each on the cheek before he turned to introduce his friend. "I'd like you both to meet my friend, Isabella."

I said hello to the girl and then waited, holding my breath. Would I hear a sweet voice, or would I hear the threatening voice I had come to dread?

Chapter 11

She smiled at both of us and it seemed like a genuine smile. "Hello, Moira. Mac, I'm glad to finally meet you. You're all Peter ever talks about."

I gasped out loud at the sound of her voice. My reaction caught everybody's attention, and I quickly tried to make light of it. "Sorry about that, someone banged my leg," I lied. "Isabella, it's wonderful to meet you, too. Listen, I don't know what I was thinking, I should've grabbed drinks for us as we walked over here. I'm heading over to the bar and to get them now—you two want anything?" With a nod and a drink order from both Peter and Isabella, I grabbed Moira's wrist and pulled her along with me, telling her she could help me carry the drinks back. As soon as we got out of hearing from Peter and Isabella, I stopped in my tracks, my eyes wide.

"Well?" Even though she asked, I had a feeling she already had the answer.

"That's not the voice I'm hearing. I don't know who this Isabella is, but I can tell that her feelings towards Peter are like dishwater compared to the voice I'm hearing. Now, what do I do?"

"For now, we get our drinks, and we go back to the table and enjoy the band. There's nothing more you can do at this point, until the voice speaks again. But this time you'll be ready for the voice, and it will be important for you to listen carefully. There might be undertones you're not hearing because of your fear. Open yourself up and listen to what the voice is really saying."

It was fine and dandy for her to go all philosophical on me, but she hadn't heard the evil in the voice like I had. And it wasn't her best friend in danger. By the time we got back to the table, the next band was playing, giving us no opportunity to talk any further. The band was fantastic, and we soon got lost in the music.

The band had started to play their last song when I felt a slight tingle in my ankle. By the time I realized what was coming, the tingle had turned to a burn, and I grasped Moira's hand under the table.

"She's here with him. I must put a stop to this. I will get rid of her."

I looked around, wildly trying to figure out where the voice had come from, but everyone there seemed to be wrapped up in the music.

"Listen carefully, Mackenzie." Moira urged as she squeezed my hand.

But I couldn't hear anything other than the hatred in the voice. Maybe I wasn't ready to hear more, or maybe I was afraid of the voice, not just for Peter, but for myself. Because what I just heard sounded like a very serious threat to my wellbeing. Somebody out there wanted Peter badly enough that they were willing to get rid of me to achieve their goal.

My instinct was to grab Peter's hand and run. I wanted to protect my best friend, and it was the first thing I thought of—his safety. But before I could act, I caught the slight shake of Moira's head. I don't know how she knew what I was thinking, but she did. I gave a sigh and shrugged my shoulders, showing her I would have patience.

Not knowing about my anxiety, Peter gave me a wink. Poor Isabella seemed oblivious to the undercurrents around her.

Moira seemed to be in my ear, telling me to listen and think about the activity going on around me. The burning in my ankle had gone from painful to a minor irritation, like an itch that needed scratching. The noise level went back to normal as well. I hadn't realized that everything had faded into the background when the voice had taken hold of me, like white noise. And the chill that had overcome me disappeared too. By the time everything came back into focus, the band had finished their encore number. "The band was great! Thank you so much for including me tonight." Moira spoke first, raising her voice over the conversations going on around us.

"Yeah, one of the best bands Ollie's has had here in a while. What did you think, Mac?"

I grinned at Peter and agreed with his assessment. There would be no sense in trying to talk to him here, and why ruin a nice evening out. I would talk to him later, in a quieter location, with Moira for backup. Besides, Isabella had no part of this and didn't need to find out that Peter's best friend heard voices in her head, and might be a little nuts.

After the band members came out to sit at the bar with the patrons, Ollie's became louder and rowdier. I invited everyone back to my place, but Isabella declined, saying she needed to get up early for a meeting. Peter at once offered to see her home and promised to stop by after he made sure Isabella had made it home safely.

But, Peter didn't keep his promise. After Moira left, I sat on my balcony, worrying about him. Peter had never broken his promises in all the years I've known him. Something was definitely wrong.

Chapter 12

Moira and I had waited for Peter to meet up with us last night. Finally, Moira said she needed to leave since she had an early morning shift at the hospital. We had joked about Peter getting caught up escorting Isabella home. But I wasn't laughing on the inside. My emotions swayed between worry and jealous anger. Was he so taken with Isabella that he would leave us hanging, or had something happened? Had the person behind the voice taken action and I missed it? One second I was reaching for my phone to call him, and the next I was tapping my foot in frustration, wanting to kick at something.

I had waited with Shaylee on the balcony for a while longer, like some pitiful homage to Juliet, before I finally admitted to myself that he wouldn't show up. As I climbed into bed, I imagined all sorts of romantic settings for Peter and Isabella. I tossed and turned all night.

———————◆———————

THE BANGING ON THE door the next morning woke me out of a sound sleep. Shaylee shot up in the air in fright. There was something ominous about that early morning pounding.

.

I stumbled out of bed and made my way to the hallway. "Hold on!" I shouted, resenting being woken by a loud pounding on my front door. Annoyed, I took my time getting my robe on before I walked to the door to open it. I don't know who I expected, but seeing a strange man standing on my front porch took my breath away.

He held his badge up in front of my face. "Mackenzie Aldkin?"

I nodded my head, confused.

"May I come in, ma'am? I have a few questions about your activities last night."

I stepped aside and motioned for him to enter. As I tied my robe around my waist a little tighter, I walked to the straight-back chair to sit, not willing to let myself get comfortable. Somehow, I had the impression I needed to keep my wits about me.

"How can I help you, officer?"

"Actually, it's Detective Byrd."

"Okay, Detective Byrd. Why are you here so early? Did something happen?"

He took his time answering me, looking around my living room as if he was searching for something, then he turned back to me. He stared me down, but I refused to be intimidated. I'd done nothing wrong that I could remember, and not even a parking ticket marred my record.

"Tell me about your activities last night, Miss Aldkin."

"I think I'd rather hear why you're here before I answer any of your questions."

My uncle would be proud of me, maybe a little lawyer blood ran through my veins too. I was beginning to get a bad feeling about this situation. I didn't know what was going on, but I would find out before I offered any information.

Detective Byrd seemed a little surprised by my answer, but he gave a slight nod of his head, and a bit of a smile touched the corner of his mouth. I don't know if I amused him, or he thought the situation funny, but I didn't appreciate the smirk.

He didn't answer me right away. He may have been trying to make me squirm, or maybe he was searching for words, but I waited him out. Two could play that game. Finally, he cleared his throat and pulled out his notebook and pen from his pocket.

"I'm investigating an attack on somebody last night. Somebody you were with. I need to get any information you might have for me."

My sudden intake of breath seemed loud, but the detective didn't notice. My thoughts jumped to Peter and his no-show last night. Was he hurt? Is that why the officer was here? I almost blurted out my questions, but I could see him assessing me and I had a feeling there was more than what he was willing to tell me.

"Yes, I went out with some friends last night."

"I think you can give me a few more details than that, Miss Aldkin."

"Not until I find out what's going on and why you're here."

It was not my nature to be combative. I was usually very cooperative. I could see that my attitude was beginning to irritate him. He hesitated for just a moment and then shrugged his shoulders before answering.

"Last night, Isabella Rossi was brutally attacked. We're trying to trace her activities for the night. Were you, or were you not, with her last night?"

I gasped out loud. The last thing I expected to hear was Isabella being attacked. She had seemed like such a sweet little thing, who would want to hurt her? I nodded my head, not knowing what to say.

"And who else was you with? Can you give me the details of how your evening went?"

I decided to cooperate. I wasn't going to play games when somebody was hurt. Yet, I still had the feeling he held something back, and it made me uneasy. I told Detective Byrd of my activities last night.

"Is Isabella okay?"

The detective looked at me straight in the eyes, not blinking and not even trying to soften his words.

"Late last night her body was found. She'd been murdered."

Chapter 13

I gasped out loud in shock. He had to be mistaken. We'd been there with her, there's no way she could be dead. What about Peter? Was he okay? And, where was he? I almost asked the questions, and then it dawned on me; the detective needed to find Isabella's murder. The last thing I should be doing was tossing out Peter's name. I told him all I remembered, but I would not speculate on anything else that might be going on with my friends. As I finished, I bit my tongue not wanting to blurt out about the voice I heard threatening us last night. At the last second, I realized there was no way to prove that I heard anything because the voice could only be heard by me. I would either come across as guilty or sounding like a crazy person, and I didn't need either one of those.

"My God, Detective Byrd, are you sure it was Isabella? I mean, of course you're sure, but how did it happen? Where did it happen? Why did it happen?"

I knew I was babbling, I didn't want the answers, but I understood I needed to hear them. My two best friends may be involved in ways I didn't understand, and I had to find out why, without dragging anybody's name into it. The detective looked at me, and he must have decided bluntness might shock me into answering him.

"She was bludgeoned to death last night outside her apartment. Around one o'clock in the morning. Where were you at that time?"

His answer shocked me enough that I didn't realize right away what his question indicated. He suspected me or at least thought I knew something about it. As his question sunk in, I realized exactly where I had been. After giving up on Peter, I was getting ready to go to bed. I had only a cat for an alibi. Deciding it would be best to be honest with him, I answered him.

"I was doing the same thing that most people are doing at one o'clock in the morning. I was in bed. I might have even been reading a book, but I'm sure I fell asleep shortly after that."

"And were you alone?"

"Of course, I was. Unless you consider my cat an eyewitness. I'm sorry, Detective, but when I left the company of my friends, I spent the rest of the evening by myself."

The man wrote in his notebook and then he asked the question I had been dreading. I knew better than to lie about this, but I sure wasn't going to offer any more information than what I had to.

"What was the exact time you left your friends? Do you have any idea where they went after you separated?"

"My friend, Moira Stewart, came back to the house with me and talked for a little bit. She left around eleven-thirty."

"And the gentleman who you also spent the evening with? What time did he leave?"

I fidgeted before I answered. I knew how damning my answer could be.

"Peter Norris did not come back to the house with us. He went with Isabella to see her home safely. We all left Ollie's around eleven."

My answer caught his attention, and he looked at me sharply to see if I was telling the truth. He let me squirm for a couple of minutes while he scribbled in his notebook.

"You're saying that Peter and Isabella left the club together? And you didn't see Peter for the rest of the night, correct?"

I could only nod my head in despair. Detective Byrd ignored my discomfort and asked me if I expected to see Peter later last night or sometime today. When I told him that yes, I expected to see him today, he nodded his head. I didn't lie, but I didn't answer his question fully.

The detective seemed satisfied with my answers and closed his notebook. Before he left, he said there may be more questions for me as the investigation developed.

I watched him walk down the porch steps, and as soon as he made it to the sidewalk, I whipped out my cell phone and dialed Peter's number. Desperate, I wanted to talk to him. There were questions to answer and the most important one—is he okay? His phone rang and rang, finally going to his voicemail. I left him a rather desperate message to call me. Placing my hands on my hips, I wondered what to do next. Common sense kicked in, and I dialed my uncle's number.

He answered on the first ring, and the concern in his voice was clear. He told me to stay where I was and not to answer the door. He explained that if the police had my name, the reporters might also have it.

After I hung up, I rushed up the stairs to get dressed. Then I made my way to the kitchen to make a pot of coffee. The smell of coffee aroma had filled the kitchen when there was a knock at the kitchen door. With a glance at the clock over the kitchen stove, I thought to myself that he had made great time.

But when I answered the door, it wasn't my Uncle Charlie, but Moira. The look of concern on her face matched mine and we held each other tightly. She knew my secret, and I wondered if she had been thinking along the same lines as me. Was the woman's voice from last night Isabella's murderer?

Chapter 14

I quickly filled her in on my morning visitor. She nodded, giving me the feeling she had been expecting this. When I finished telling her about the questions Detective Byrd had asked, she explained why she was there.

"I was doing my rounds with the doctors when I overheard one talking about a new case that had just been brought into the morgue. The hair stood on the back of my neck and I knew, I just knew, somehow, we were all connected to it. I made some lame excuse and got out of the rest of my rounds and hurried down to the morgue to find out what was happening. The coroner told me about his newest arrival and the circumstances that had brought her there. And then he told me her name."

Moira's announcement made it seem all that much more real. Talks of coroner and morgues were not something that came up in my daily conversations. Before I could ask her if she had any other details, Uncle Charlie walked in.

My uncle was a serious man, not prone to show emotion in front of other people. Probably because he always had to keep his emotions in check while in the courtroom, but today he hid nothing. He took me by the shoulders, looking deep in my eyes to make sure I was okay. Something he saw seemed to relieve him because he pulled me in close for a bear hug, tight enough that I could barely breathe. After a few reassuring moments, I assured him I was okay and then he turned to say hello to Moira.

I was surprised to see the two of them studying each other. I knew that they both wanted to take care of me. But that was ridiculous, I was a grown woman and perfectly able to take care of myself. Besides, the one needing care right now was Peter.

"Come on you two, let's head into the kitchen. I haven't had a cup of coffee yet, and I can't function until I get some caffeine in me."

Uncle Charlie pulled a chair out for Moira, always the perfect gentleman. I grabbed the mugs and the entire pot of coffee and set them in the middle of the table. We each prepared our own cup and then sat back, ready to work. Like a family, we sat around the table, coffee in hand trying to figure out the problem in front of us. Uncle Charlie knew Peter as well as I did. He was part of my extended family, and he had watched the two of us grow up together. Secretly, I think my uncle was aware of my love for Peter. Although he never told me he knew, I was pretty sure he would wholly approve if the two of us got involved in something deeper than friendship.

"What I can't understand is what happened to Peter last night. If he says he's going to meet me, then you can be sure it's going to happen. What if he was involved in Isabella's attack?"

Moira and my uncle looked at me like I was crazy. Neither one of them could comprehend I would say something like that about Peter. I saw their expression and hurried to explain what I meant.

"No, no. I don't mean he did the attack! But what if he got hurt, trying to defend her, or something like that? You know, as well as I do, Uncle Charlie, that Peter would go down fighting to defend someone, regardless of how he might be hurt. What if he's lying on the side of the road somewhere hurt, or worse?" I could feel myself getting tensed up and anxious as I spoke. The words made sense, but I somehow didn't feel Peter was hurt. I sensed he was okay, and that there had to be a reasonable explanation for what happened the night before.

"Mac, if the police are looking for Peter for questioning, they're searching everywhere. If he was lying around somewhere hurt, they would have found him. You can cross that possibility off the list."

"So, the police are looking for Peter?" Moira wanted confirmation of what she hadn't been able to say, and she looked to Uncle Charlie for that.

"I'd bet there is a one-hundred percent possibility they are looking for him. This Detective Byrd was here this morning, fishing for information from Mac. That means he hasn't found him yet. We need to find him before they do. Have you tried to call him?"

I explained that all I had been getting was a ring tone. His home phone wasn't being picked up either. While I was answering him, Charlie picked up a pad of paper he found on the counter, pulled the pen out of his shirt pocket and got poised to write.

"We need to come up with a list of people and places we can check out and see if he's been there in the last eight to twelve hours. Find out if any of his other friends have any idea of where he is, or if they have any information on what happened last night."

I agreed with Charlie, and as I gave him some names and numbers, Moira refilled our coffee cups.

I was distracted but noticed Shaylee had walked over to me a couple of times and circled my chair as if looking for attention. But now wasn't the time to be playing with her, so I ignored her. She looked at me with disgust, as if I was a simpleton and then tried one more time. When I still ignored her, she jumped up on the table and put her face right next to mine and meowed at me; a rather shrill urgent sound. Finally, getting my attention, she jumped down from the table and walked to the front room, where she jumped up on the window seat and paced in front of the window.

I shrugged my shoulders, but Moira would not let me get off that easily, and she gestured towards the living room with her index finger, her meaning clear. I pushed the chair back and got up, annoyed that my train of thought was being interrupted.

I walked over to the window seat and reached for the cat when she meowed again. Then I saw what was going on out in front of my house.

It was like something out of a two-bit cops-and-robbers show. There were five or six police cars with their lights flashing, blocking a car that was parked in my driveway. Police officers were crouched beside their cars, pointing their weapons at a man standing on my porch.

"Uncle Charlie, come quick," I yelled. I raced to the front door and threw it open. The detective warned his men not to shoot. He was putting handcuffs on Peter by the time Uncle Charlie and Moira arrived by my side.

"Counselor, Mackenzie." He acknowledged the two of us, looking curiously at Moira. It was then I realized my uncle knew Detective Byrd, maybe from a past case.

"Are you arresting Peter?" I asked, my heart in my throat.

"Not at this point. We're taking him down to the station for some questions. He agreed to come calmly and be cooperative."

"Then why the handcuffs?"

The detective gave a shrug, but when he saw that I was getting ready to argue and make a fuss, he signaled to the officer next to him to remove the cuffs from Peter's wrists.

That's all my uncle needed to hear. In an instant, he changed from the easy-going uncle to the foreboding lawyer. He instructed Peter not to say anything until he arrived at the station. He told Detective Byrd that he was Peter's lawyer and wanted to be present at his questioning. I could see the detective wasn't happy about Peter's instant counsel on hand, but there was nothing he could do about it.

"He'll be in the interrogation room waiting for your arrival, counselor." With those final words, the detective and his entourage were gone, and my front yard looked normal again.

"Mackenzie, I'm going right now. You two meet me there. Between the three of us, we need to get this sorted out. There's no reason for Peter to be in an interrogation room."

Charlie didn't even wait for an answer, he left just as fast as the police had.

I decided I didn't need to waste any time either. With barely a word to Moira, I ran upstairs to get dressed. When I came back downstairs, Moira informed me she would drive and handed me my purse.

It wasn't until we are a few blocks from the police station that I happened to look down at my phone and I saw a missed call from Peter. He must've tried to call me last night, and I had not heard it. I pushed my cell on speaker, so Moira could listen in.

"Hey Mac, it's me, Peter. Listen, my phone is almost dead, and my car *is* dead. I dropped Isabella off and I was on my way back to your place when I got a flat tire. I called roadside assistance, and I'm waiting for them to show up. Don't wait up for me, I'm sure this is going to take a while. I'll just go home from here when they get the car fixed."

I saw that Peter's call had come in almost forty-five minutes before Isabella had been murdered. Peter had an alibi. I breathed a big sigh of relief. I needed to get this information to the detective as fast as possible. Moira seemed to have the same idea because I felt her push on the car's accelerator, and she weaved in and out of traffic to get us there. When we pulled up to the main entrance of the station with a squeal of tires, Moira was quick to tell me to get inside as fast as I could.

I didn't waste any time arguing with her, I had the door open before she even came to a complete stop. I raced up the front stairs, waited impatiently to be scanned through security, and then walked to the front desk, demanding to see Detective Byrd.

Apparently, the detective heard my rather loud demand, and he came out of the backroom. I rushed forward and thrust my phone in his face.

"Here's Peter's alibi, proof that he was nowhere near Isabella when she was killed!" I said triumphantly.

The detective looked at me and then at the phone inches from his nose. I swear he was disappointed that he didn't have a solid case. To give him credit, he took the phone into the back with him and said he'd listen to the message in the presence of Peter and Uncle Charlie.

Detective Byrd, Uncle Charlie, and Peter came out of the backroom and met us at the front desk. Peter still had a dazed look, his eyes wide and his tan looked a few shades lighter, but when he saw me, he broke into a big grin. Rushing to my side, he picked me up and swung me around in a big hug. He had a huge grin for Moira too. When the detective said something to him, Peter just looked at the man, shrugged his shoulders, holding out his hands to show that there were no hard feelings. Uncle Charlie told Peter he would handle the paperwork, so the three of us should go ahead and leave. I don't know if he feared we would say something that would incriminate ourselves, or if he simply wanted to make sure every "t" was crossed and "i" dotted.

We were a jovial trio as we walked out of the courthouse. And because of that, the tension in the air hit me without warning, almost knocking the breath out of my lungs. I felt myself go into a fog, the hair stood up on the back of my neck, and that darn scar tingled to the point of pain.

"It's not fair. It should be me celebrating with him. Peter, when will you realize that we belong together?"

Chapter 15

The voice came out of nowhere, with no warning. No storm set it off, and I instantly longed-for Shaylee to comfort me. I found myself aware of differences this time. I could clearly decipher not only the forlorn tone from the voice but also the anger. I pulled myself out of the fog that my brain wrapped itself in and took a hurried glance around me. The voice sounded so clear, the woman must be close by.

My eyes darted from one thing to the next, looking for somebody hiding or looking suspicious. I swore my head must have looked as if it was rotating like a woman possessed. I didn't notice anyone who stood out.

"Hey Mac, you're trailing behind, what's up? You okay?"

Moira glanced back at me, raising her eyebrows when she saw the look on my face. The tingly feelings were suddenly gone. My biggest concern became clear: was the person behind the voice harmful, or just forlornly in love with Peter? If that was the case, I could relate.

Peter stepped back and grabbed my hand. Before we could go more than two steps, Moira stopped. She looked at me firmly and spoke with an authoritative voice.

"Mackenzie, this cannot go any farther without Peter and your uncle understanding what's going on with you." She held her palm up to my face when I started to say something. "No arguments Mackenzie. You're not crazy, and other people need to understand what you are experiencing."

Instinctively I knew it to be futile to argue with her. I remained quiet when we got back to her car, and as we climbed in, I again tried to imagine how to tell everybody what had been going on. And even more, how would Peter react? Would he trust me or just consider me nuts? Would this repel him away from me? There was no doubt that my uncle would believe me. Uncle Charlie had seen too many things in his life, both as a lawyer and as a traveler. He wouldn't question, he would simply accept.

The drive back to my house seemed unusually quiet as we each contemplated our own thoughts. I think Peter was still in shock, his color still hadn't fully returned, and his silence spoke louder than words, over his close call of being considered a murder suspect. At Moira's insistence, I was sitting in the backseat with Peter, and his closeness gave me comfort. I hoped he was feeling the same. At one point, my ankle twinged and I reached down absentmindedly to rub it.

"Here," Peter said, as he pulled my feet up on his lap and gently rubbed them. As his fingers ran across my scar, it seemed as if it radiated a static heat. I closed my eyes and enjoyed his touch.

We didn't have to wait long for Uncle Charlie to arrive. Apparently, Detective Byrd was happy to get rid of him. The detective seemed disappointed Uncle Charlie had cleared Peter so quickly. And, unfortunately, there were no active clues for them to follow.

But we had an active clue, we just needed to figure out what to do with it.

After Uncle Charlie finished filling us in, I knew the time had come for me to tell them about the voices. I cleared my throat nervously, hoping that they would accept what I said.

"The lightning strike did more to me than leave a scar on my ankle. I seem to be able to connect with other people when they are at an elevated level of stress." Blurting it out seemed to be the easiest way to start.

"Mac, you've always been in tune with other people's feelings, that shouldn't make it any different."

I looked at Peter and gave him a weak smile. "It's more than just understanding their feelings, Peter. I actually hear their words in my head."

Uncle Charlie and Moira exchanged looks.

"I'm not hearing complete conversations, and it's not all the time. I hear the voice when there seems to be a lot of tension—either in the air or possibly from the person talking. What comes to me is their most emphasized part of the conversation. The part they're most passionate about seems to come across in my head. But, it's not only the words; I feel their emotions. And Peter, last night at Ollie's, a voice made a threat against us. I assumed I was the one the voice referred to. I never guessed she spoke about Isabella."

After a stunned moment of silence from Peter and my uncle, they both began asking questions. At first, I cringed, but Moira reached out and gave my hand a squeeze of encouragement. That simple touch gave me courage. I took a deep breath as I told them all that had happened since the lightning bolt struck the sand next to me.

When I finished, we all stared at Peter, hoping he'd be able to tell us who the voice belonged to that was penetrating my thoughts. But he looked as lost as I felt.

"I can't imagine who this woman would be, Mac. The only one that I had been dating on and off was Isabella, and that's why I wanted you to meet her last night. I honestly can't even tell you that I have deep feelings for her. So, whoever this woman is, she's jealous for no reason."

Before he spoke, Uncle Charlie looked over at me, taking everything in, including the relief I must have shown on my face when Peter said he hadn't been serious about Isabella.

"This woman obviously doesn't understand your feelings, Peter. At some point, you've connected with her, and she's built much more out of that connection in her mind than it means. We need to figure out who she is before anything else happens. Mackenzie, why did you think it was you she was threatening?"

"I don't know, I guess, just because Peter and I are always together."

"Exactly. And if your thoughts went that way so quickly, eventually hers are going to, as well. Especially since she's already eliminated one rival for Peter's attention. So, the way I look at it, she's either going to go after you, or she'll get mad at Peter and go after him. You're both in danger. But we have an advantage. We're one step ahead of her. The disadvantage is that we don't know who she is. Yet."

In true lawyer-like fashioned, my uncle laid the facts out for us. Now we needed to take the next step to protect ourselves and stop this woman.

Chapter 16

Uncle Charlie walked over to my desk, grabbing a pad of paper, and tossed it to Peter.

"Peter, I want you to write down any dates you've had in the last year. Then list any casual get-togethers where you may have met someone new. Try to be as specific as possible; we need details, like where you were and who else might have been with you. Maybe if we knew the circumstances of the meeting, we might understand how this woman became so infatuated with you."

I had to hide my smile. Peter looked embarrassed. He was a popular guy, and I was sure this would be interesting. I leaned forward, ready to tease,

"Mackenzie, why don't we go out to the garden? I want to work with you on a few exercises that should help you read the changes around you before you hear a voice. If you can concentrate more on the circumstances, than the voice, then we might have an advantage." I hesitated before getting to my feet. I didn't want to miss the chance to give Peter a few teasing barbs. But Moira wasn't letting up and urged me out the French doors and into my garden. Shaylee followed close behind us.

Once we were outside, she shut the doors firmly behind her and ordered me to find my favorite spot and go stand in the middle of it. That was easy enough, and without hesitation I walked over to the small Gazebo located in the seclusion of the back corner of the garden. I had to walk down a step-stone path, almost hidden by the ground orchids and ferns I allowed to grow with abandonment. Shaylee stood by her usual post at the foot of the pathway, where she often spent time pacing back and forth. More than once I had teased her that she looked like a guard, keeping the creatures of the garden from getting too close to the entry to the house. Silly, but the swish of her tail reminded me of guards walking their post at a castle gate.

"Okay, I'm here, now what?" I called back to Moira.

"Survey your surroundings, take in all your view. Note what stands out to you." There was something about Moira's voice that was compelling. Even though we were at opposite ends of the walkway, it was as if she was right beside me, speaking in her normal soft voice. I cringed when I compared my loudness to her gentleness.

She waited patiently for me to get serious and follow her instructions. I twitched my shoulders and stood a bit taller, taking on the appearance of concentration. I moved my head in a slow, even motion, taking in the surrounding garden. It was as if I saw it with new eyes. The first thing that caught my attention were the colors. I hadn't realized how much of the charm from my garden was due to the riot of color. It was like a box of crayons had exploded in my small garden. Shades of colors draped over top of the green foliage, which acted as a backdrop, it was hard to say which color was more predominate. A wave of cheerfulness engulfed me, and I was almost lighthearted.

Then a movement to my right caught my eye, and I turned my head in that direction to watch the birds come and go from the feeder I had hung from a post. The positioning was supposed to deter the squirrels, but I'm sure they took it as a challenge. I must be honest-I get as much enjoyment from watching the squirrels as I do the birds. A brilliant red Cardinal flew from the feeder to the wind chime hanging from a lower branch in the old oak tree. As the wind blew, the metal of the chimes hit each other, ringing out its own song.

Another slight movement of my head and my focus was drawn to the oversized birdbath Peter had given me on my last birthday. The sunlight reflected off the surface, intensifying the gleam of the water. Moira's voice instructed me to see beyond the obvious and I noticed the shadows created by the overhead trees and foliage. As the breeze moved the branches, the shadows shifted, and I could find smaller plants, long ago planted and forgotten, claiming their own stake in the garden. I smiled to myself as a little rabbit looked up at me. I could almost imagine his guilt at being caught nipping on one of my plants.

Without my being aware, Moira had walked to stand by my side. Her voice, so close, startled me for a second.

"Now close your eyes. Experience your surroundings. Be aware of more than the sounds. What else is going on around you?"

I closed my eyes to the sights I was enjoying and held my breath for a moment. I identified the sounds that I expected—the birds, wind chimes, music coming from my outdoor speakers—and released my breath, breathing normally. As I listened, I began to pick out the subtler sounds around me. The leaves moving in the wind, the distant barking of a dog, the slamming of a car door, and the street outside the courtyard. I almost felt myself sway as I picked up the sounds of a bee working hard amongst the blossoms, and the tree frog, angry at our intrusion.

I became aware of the sun on my head, as droplets of sweat formed between my shoulder blades and ran down to the small of my back, to be absorbed into the waistband of my shorts. My nose twitched from the sweet smell of Gardenia, and I jumped when a leaf from the tree above me landed on my arm.

Then Moira made a hissing sound, entirely out of sync with everything else I had just experienced. I don't know how she did it, but she made the sound seem threatening, and I noted the physical change I experienced. The hair stood to attention on my neck, my muscles tightened, and I drew my breath in sharply. But then a heat began to build around my ankle, followed by a coolness. The coldness moved at a snail's pace, tracing the exact path that my scar made.

I opened my eyes in shock. Never have I been more aware of my body and its reactions. Moira didn't ask me the obvious, perfectly aware her little exercise had worked. More than that, I'd picked up on what signs to watch for within myself. With a pleased nod, she moved to sit on the seat gazebo and patted the space next to her.

We sat in silence for a moment before I asked, "Where did you learn to make that hissing sound?"

"Oh, that's just something I use to chase away a nuisance."

"Well, I'd run if you made it at me. That was creepy, Moira."

"Sometimes, you need to be a bit assertive and frighten the pests away."

If I hadn't been watching her closely, I would have missed the glance she sent to Shaylee. The cat seemed to read something in the glance, and she got up and walked over to a corner of the gazebo. Her tail flicked a couple of times as she intently stared into the underbrush. Moira reached over to pat my hand in comfort, and her action distracted me enough to doubt what I thought I saw. It was a quick, blurred movement, right at Shaylee's eye level. The cat reached up with one paw and seemed to bat at the movement, but I didn't notice her connect with anything. It must have been a trick of the light coming through the canopy of foliage above us. Before I could dwell on it, Moira distracted me with a question.

"Can you remember what you experienced when I hissed at you? And still remember everything you observed before that? You will need to practice this over and over until you are doing it without being aware that you are. Hopefully, the next time you hear a voice, you will be able to pinpoint what is going on around you and anticipate the physical reaction you will have."

"Yes. I'm willing to try. But how is this going to help?"

Moira thought for a moment, scratching the cat's ears when she jumped up between the two of us and then continued.

"I believe if you are fully aware of what is going on around you, then when the voice comes, you will also be able to pick up on the vibes of its surroundings. I don't know how to put it into words that will explain it to you."

"Don't worry, I think you just did. And I understand what you are saying. This makes it easier to deal with hearing the voices in my head, so. I can prepare for the next time. Hopefully, that will help us find out who this woman is and what she plans next."

I got to my feet with determination, I had a purpose to achieve. We had to figure out who killed Isabella and was so fixated on Peter.

"Let's find out what kind of list Peter managed to come up with for Uncle Charlie."

As we walked back to the house, I realized the woman beside me had done precisely what she had planned. I wasn't merely walking up a pathway, I was also taking in the sights and sounds of the surrounding area.

Chapter 17

Peter and Uncle Charlie were going over his list back inside the house, but their conversation came to a halt as we walked in. Peter tried to cover the paper, so I couldn't read what was on it, but he wasn't fast enough. There was a significant list on both sides of the paper.

"You, Casanova you!" Flicking his earlobe as I had when we were kids, I sat down next to him and pulled the pad of paper away from him.

Two columns were facing me, one with the heading 'Dated' and the other 'Friends.' I was pleased to note the column for dating wasn't overwhelming. It was a little disheartening to find my name at the top of the list for friends. I sighed and consoled myself with the fact that "MAC" was in caps, and it appeared to have been re-written many times, the heavy thickness of ink making it stand out from anything else on the page.

"You know, I think I know most of these names, at least under the friend heading." Letting my finger run down the column, I read over the list. "I can't picture any of these girls making threats, or killing Isabella in a fit of jealous rage."

"Tell us about the date names. Any unusual behavior from them? Maybe too possessive or clingy?" Uncle Charlie suggested, accepting my judgment about the girls we both knew.

Blushing in embarrassment, Peter hesitated before he answered. I was pretty sure I knew what he was thinking; it was one thing to talk about his dates with the guys, or even me, but something different saying it to my uncle.

"Go ahead, Peter, no one's here to pass judgment. We've all had dates. Besides, this isn't just about you—it's about finding who's a killer." Uncle Charlie's words loosened Peter's vocal cords, and he went down the list one name at a time.

I let Moira and my uncle listen to the words. I was too busy concentrating on the emotion in Peter's voice as he spoke of the different women and the dates he had had with them. The tension in my shoulders lessened as he continued. Most of the dates had been causal, often fixed up by one of his friends or as a double date. There were only two girls that Peter had gone out with several times, Brenda and Faye. Peter smiled as he told us about the dates he'd had with those two, but there didn't seem to be any deep emotion, dreaminess, or passion in his voice. As he talked, I remembered that he had spoken about Isabella the same way. I realized Peter had not found the love of his life in these women. I smiled slightly, there was still hope.

"What do you think, Mac?" I looked up to find the others waiting for my response. I had been so intent on listening to the tone of Peter's voice, I hadn't heard Uncle Charlie asking me the question.

"Sorry, I was thinking about Isabella."

My smile faltered when I saw Peter's haunted expression. It was clear to me that he was blaming himself for Isabella's murder. I understood what I said next could make an enormous difference. It would either ease his mind or pile on the guilt.

"Peter, it's not about what I think, or what you think, either. It's about the killer's perception of your feelings towards these women. Personally, I agree. Not one of these dates seems serious enough to warrant such jealousy. But whoever is out there, the one whose voice I've heard has claimed you as her personal property, and she will fight to keep you to herself. She's already killed to accomplish this. She's deranged, and until we figure it out, dangerous."

Moira and Uncle Charlie nodded their heads in agreement. I hesitated and then continued, not sure if what I had to say would make any sense. Even to me, it seemed a little farfetched.

"Something deep down inside is telling me it will not be as easy as simply taking a look at the women you've dated. You would have picked up on her intensity. After all, you're not an insensitive jerk who doesn't pay attention to a woman when you're with them. And I would have noticed." Realizing that he could take my last comment in a couple of different ways, I coughed to cover my unease.

"You might have something there, Mac." Uncle Charlie agreed with me, not even noticing my discomfort. Deciding to listen to my own words—it was about who killed Isabella, nothing more—I pushed the paperback in front of Peter.

"You're not done. We need to list your casual friends too, maybe someone you met in passing, maybe a co-worker, or a waitress. Think Peter, it's someone that's on the edge of your day-to-day life. Someone looking in, who wants desperately to be a part of your life."

Peter understood and picked up the pen to write. Uncle Charlie coached him, offering suggestions of who to think about for the list. The two men played off each other, like a pair of chess players, matching suggestions to names.

"Start with your daily routine, Peter. Who do you meet on your way to work?"

Peter wrote down more names.

Charlie and Peter moved down their list, now concentrating on Peter's co-workers. I watched Peter write longhand and admired his penmanship. I also noticed how strong his hands looked, and I wondered how they would feel touching me the way a lover would, not a friend. Peter looked up at me with a smile, and I quickly looked away, hoping he couldn't read where my thoughts were going.

Enough of this mooning, I told myself. I needed to do something constructive. I listened as Moira asked Peter a question about someone he might have known and that gave me an idea. Nudging Peter's arm, I asked for a piece of paper. Grabbing a pen from my junk drawer, I sat down at the table and wrote my own list of names.

"I'm doing a list too. Maybe, if we compared them when we're done, we might find someone we both unknowingly had contact with. Someone we both talk to each day, even if we are only saying hi, then it might be a starting point to work from."

"That's a clever idea, Mackenzie. We need to try everything we can," Moira said as she stroked Shaylee's tail. The gray kitten was sitting contently on her lap, watching our every move. She acted as if she understood the conversation going on around her, as she turned her head towards each of us as we spoke.

We pondered and jotted down names for a while. I knew Peter, he was blaming himself for Isabella's death. I understood because I was blaming myself: if only I had figured out where the voice was coming from, I might have been clearer on what her intentions were and could have prevented it.

Guilt could be a funny thing. It can slow you down and make you indecisive, dwelling in it. Or it can spur you on to find a solution. Thankfully Peter and I were both determined to help prevent any more attacks and bring this woman to justice.

We finished at about the same time, and both breathed a sigh of relief. It was surprising how taxing the task had been, but we both had a complete list, and nobody had been left out. Now the list needed to be compared for similarities. I needed a break from sitting for so long, so I pushed the papers to Uncle Charlie.

"Okay, we've done our part. Now I'm letting you examine this with Moira to see if there are any matches from the two lists. Then from there, we can concentrate on what to do next."

Moira moved over to sit next to Uncle Charlie and I looked at Peter, pointing to the front door.

"Are you up for a walk, Peter? I need to stretch my legs and think about nothing for a couple of minutes."

He lost no time getting to his feet and, and we headed to the beach. We didn't talk about it, we simply walked that way. We were comfortable enough with each other that we didn't need words, and we walked shoulder to shoulder. Occasionally somebody would pass by and say hello. I found myself carefully surveying them, wondering. I saw Peter was too. It's an awful experience to look at people you know and wonder if there's something wrong with them, something evil.

Before we knew it, we were back at the same spot on the beach where everything had started. There wasn't a cloud in the sky, and it was a beautiful day with no sign of rain, or storms, or anything terrible. The tension left my shoulders as I breathed in the salty air, letting it fill my lungs and clear my head.

This was precisely what I needed. I plopped down on the sand next to Peter and we watched the waves crash against the shoreline in comfortable silence. There were people in your life where words are not necessary, and there was no reason to chatter all the time; Peter was one of those people for me.

I don't know how long we sat there before I heard the voices calling me. At first, I feared it was in my head, but then Peter answered, and I looked over to find two lifeguards walking in our direction.

"Hey, you two. How you doing, Mac? I've haven't seen you on the beach since your accident. I hope you suffered no ill effects."

Peter and I exchanged guilty looks before I answered the young lifeguard, thanking her for her concern. She was a pretty thing, taller than me, with traditional long blonde hair. I looked at her companion, equally tan and muscular, and tried to figure out what he held wrapped in a towel. He was handling it gently, as if it might easily break.

"I'm doing good, Karen, thanks for asking. Slow day here on the beach for you and Roger, isn't it?"

"That's the way we like it. Let people enjoy the beach and keep us sitting in our towers," Karen answered, chuckling.

"We saw the two of you sitting here, so we took a break and brought this for you, Mac."

Roger held the curious object out, laughing at the expression on my face.

"It won't hurt you, it's actually pretty cool. This is what happens when lightning hits the sand: it creates this piece of structure, it's almost artwork. It's called a fulgurite. We saved this piece for you because it was from your lightning strike."

Peter took it from Roger before I could reach for it and pulled the towel back to reveal what, at first glance, looked like a chunky piece of bleached coral. I peered at it carefully and noticed that it resembled the scarring on my ankle. Most of it was still coarse and rough looking, but I could see where crystallization had started. The crystallized pieces were in the shape of coral, with a delicate feathery design.

It was beautiful, and I felt drawn to it. I couldn't explain why, but I reached my hands out for it. As soon as I touched it, I felt like I was going into a trance. Everything around me seemed intensified. I felt the molecules of sand hit my skin, and the wind seemed to move me, even though I was still firmly in place. The sun seemed to burn brighter on my shoulders, and I clearly heard every noise around me.

The sounds were so clear, they almost seemed to take on colors. Green for the easy-going tones from my friends beside me, blue for the sound of the gentle surf hitting the shore, and reds for the angry calls of the seagulls. When Peter spoke, I saw many colors, as his tone carried questions about what they brought, happiness at seeing our friends, and calmness from sitting at the beach. As the colors blended in front of my eyes, words penetrated my thoughts, and I came out of my daze. My fingers gently traced the pattern running through the fulgurite.

If I had thought I was strongly affected by it through the towel, I was not at all prepared for what happened when I touched it head-on. It was like being hit by lightning all over again. Intensifying my whole being, but without the pain. At first, I drew my hand away, but then I reached back out and touched it again. Somehow, I sensed if I handled it for too long, it would be an overload.

I heard Karen say they needed to get back to their tower, and watched Peter wrap the lightning rock back into the towel. As he wrapped it up, a small piece snapped off the end, and Peter caught it before it hit the ground. After they left, Peter and I headed back home. I needed to talk to Moira about what had just happened. I didn't understand it, but I knew she would have the answers for me.

Chapter 18

My discussion with Moira had to wait.

"This isn't going to be good," Peter mumbled when we both noticed an unfamiliar car in my driveway.

We saw Detective Byrd standing at the front window of my living room, looking out. I had hoped we were done with the man, but I guess that wasn't going to be. Smiling at Peter, I tried to reassure him.

"Well, no matter what happens, at least your lawyer's here for you." I gave a weak laugh, realizing the joke wasn't all that funny. "There's nothing to worry about, Peter. We've done nothing wrong. The detective is probably only trying to do his job, and I'm sure he's got more questions. Because, somehow, I don't imagine he's caught the killer yet."

Peter nodded and straightened his shoulders as he walked to the front door.

"Detective Byrd dropped in to ask if we had remembered any other details that might help the investigation," Uncle Charlie said. "He assured me, Peter, that you're not under any suspicion, so go ahead and answer his questions. That goes for you too, Mac. I'm sure we all want to find Isabella's killer and put this behind us."

I knew my uncle well, and I heard the warning in his voice. It was clear to me that he was telling us to answer the detective's questions but offer no other information. To be honest, that was fine with me. There was no way I wanted to tell an officer of the law I was hearing voices, and the voices belonged to the killer. He would never believe me. And honestly, how could I expect him to? I still had a tough time believing.

The detective gave a friendly smile. "I realize I asked you these questions before, but I hoped that after thinking about this for a few hours, you might have come up with some additional details. Does anything stick out in your mind as being odd or out of the ordinary at Ollie's last night? Did you see anybody who stood out in any way? Somebody who wasn't part of any group or seem overly interested in your table, particularly Isabella? Any little bit like that would be helpful."

He looked at us hopefully, but we couldn't give him what he wanted. We'd seen nothing out of the ordinary, and that was the truth.

I had to give the man credit, he was dogged in his questioning. Repeating and rewording the questions, as if that would trigger something in our memory, but we couldn't give him the answers he was looking for. Finally, he shrugged his shoulders and getting to his feet, gave each of us his card.

"Listen, if you think of anything, be sure to call me right away. The smallest detail might be important."

He turned back to my uncle and Moira and wished them both a good day before he left, with almost a dejected hunch to his stance.

It wasn't until his car was gone from sight that we all felt relieved. Uncle Charlie was the first to break the silence.

"The two of you did well. You answered his questions, giving no extra information. Now, we need to get to work."

Peter and I nodded our heads in agreement and sat down again at the table. Moira pushed a piece of paper towards us.

"Charlie and I went over both of your lists a few times. We came up with three names that were on both lists. It gives us a start, even if we've missed someone," Moira said

Before I got a closer view of the list, Peter took it from my hands, looking it over himself. I saw him nod as he recognized the names, but I saw no spark of emotion. These women were only casual acquaintances to him, I could tell at once, and I sighed with relief. It would be much easier to investigate the three women if I didn't have it in the back of my head that Peter was romantically interested in them.

"Yeah, you're right. This first one here on the list, Judy Nick, she's the waitress at the coffee shop. You guys must have seen her around, too. Can't picture her killing somebody, though. She's afraid of her own shadow."

Mentally, I pictured Judy Nick. She was a pretty girl who hid behind huge glasses and barely spoke unless you talked to her first. I had to be honest, I agreed with Peter. The few times I had spoken to Judy, she had come across as an intelligent woman but shy.

The next name on the list we both recognized, but Peter had a bit of a problem remembering where he had met her. I had to remind him.

"Peter, we don't see Gloria Viola every day, but we do see her a couple times a week. She's the artist that often has her easel set up on the Boardwalk. You know, the one with the dark hair and the short shorts. She paints landscapes and occasionally does quick sketches of the kids playing on the beach."

"Oh yeah, I remember Gloria. Talented girl and she loves to talk. I never understood how she can carry on a conversation while she's painting. You'd think she would need as much concentration as possible." Peter laughed as he remembered who I was talking about and her talent for multitasking.

The next woman on the list neither one of us had any problems remembering. Melissa Gray owned a small general store. You could buy anything from stamps, food, or last-minute beach equipment there. She also sold the best homemade ice cream in the area. Melissa knew everybody, and everybody knew her. The thought of her having a malicious bone in her body was laughable. She was interested in anybody who came into her store and often got their entire life story out of them without them even being aware of it. Overweight from, as she put it, sampling the ice cream to make sure the flavors were right, and with a personality that easily made you forget her size, Melissa was the least likely of the three suspects.

"Really, Uncle Charlie? Melissa Gray? You know her as well as the rest of us. Can you picture her murdering somebody in cold blood?"

"I agree with you, Mac, but we had to put any possibilities down on that paper. At least it gives us a working point."

"Well, great, there are three names, but now what do we do with them?" Peter asked, frustration ringing from his voice.

There was silence for a moment after his question, and I glanced at the other two, wondering what was happening. It took Uncle Charlie a moment before he cleared his throat and a moment later did it again. It was clear he was nervous about what he was about to say, which was unusual. Sensing his unease, Moira answered Peter's question for him.

"We've come up with a plan Peter, one you and Mac will need to agree to, but if it works, the killer will come out in the open where we can set a trap and catch her." She paused for a moment, making sure she had our attention before continuing.

"Since jealousy is the factor that brings this woman's emotions to a boiling point, we need to play on that. Remember, her emotions must be brought out so that Mackenzie can hear her voice again."

I gave Moira a frown, interrupting her brilliant train of thought. "Wait. Can't we simply get each of them to say something, and I'll recognize her voice?"

"In theory, that should work, but I bet the woman's voice changes with her emotions. And each time you heard the voice, she was highly emotional. She may put up a big front during her every normal interaction with other people. I see this repeatedly in the courtroom when someone is so highly agitated. They sound completely different from a normal conversation," explained Uncle Charlie. He motioned to Moira to continue.

"What we believe would work best is for you two to become a couple."

"What?" Peter and I both spat the word out at the same time, taken by surprise at her suggestion.

Moira looked at both of us and smiled. I glanced at Uncle Charlie and saw him grinning. It was obvious he approved of this plan, and that was great, but I wasn't sure how I felt about it. I needed more details.

"Yes, a couple. Peter, you need to take Mackenzie out on a few dates, very public dates. And you need to romance her. You need to make this mystery woman jealous," Moira suggested.

Uncle Charlie picked Moira's explanation and continued.

"The idea is to be in public, to draw her out. We will be in the background, watching you. Then, when she makes her move, we'll be there to catch her."

Peter and I exchanged looks. It might be different if the plan came from us, but it didn't sound right coming from somebody else. It felt as if we were being pimped out and used as live bait.

"But what if Mac doesn't hear the voice in time and whoever this woman is, attacks her? How can we watch Mac twenty-four hours a day? I mean, the killer must have caught Isabella unawares. I don't know if I like this," Peter added as he rubbed his chin, his hands slightly shaking.

We became quiet as we contemplated Peter's question. Knowing he was worried about me felt good, but of course, this situation needed our full attention, and we had to do something.

"The difference between Isabella and me is that I won't be unaware, Peter." I reached out and lightly touched his arm. "I will know when she's coming because she'll tell me."

Chapter 19

I had to admit, the idea of being Peter's date had definite benefits. Holding hands, maybe a stolen kiss, who knew where this would lead. I was starting to feel cautiously excited about the plan.

"All right, then let's get to work," Uncle Charlie said as he rubbed his hands gleefully. My uncle loved to plan and plot. Details were what he lived for, and without waiting for any of us to reply, he pulled the pad of paper Peter had been using and tore off the sheet he had written on. In seconds, he made an agenda for Peter and me to begin our 'dating life'.

"I hate to burst your bubble, Uncle Charlie, but Peter and I have been friends for so long I don't think anyone would buy the idea that we're finally dating," I said, *regardless of how much I had secretly hoped for it*, I added in my mind.

"Oh, I don't think it will be that hard of a leap for people to make," Moira said, as I caught the slight wink, that only I could see. "After all, as I understand it, you and Peter have been spending time together for years and I think any person with a bit of romance in them will put two and two together. Now you two just need to play it up and make it realistic so people will accept it."

Before I replied, Peter jumped in to agree with Moira, playfully reaching over to grab my hand. "Come on, Mac, it can't be that hard to imagine being my girlfriend, is it?"

I knew I was blushing at his question, and I looked anywhere except at him, so he wouldn't notice.

"Of course, it isn't," Uncle Charlie answered for me, "anybody with a brain would be able to see the natural progression of your friendship. We need to capitalize on this, and we need to get moving fast." He got up, pointed to his chair it and then pointed at me. "The two of you need to get in the habit of being cozy with each other, so get over here and sit next to Peter. We'll start practicing right now."

Everyone giggled at Uncle Charlie's antics of pretending he was a drill sergeant, as I sat down next to Peter. He pulled me in for a hug and grinned, showing his dimples. He kept his arm over my shoulder as we listened to Uncle Charlie's plan of action. As he talked, I sneaked a look at Peter, and he caught my glance. He absentmindedly kissed my forehead.

I caught Uncle Charlie winking at Moira as he straightened himself up, and grinning from ear-to-ear, he turned to us. "So, the first thing we need to do is figure out how and when your paths cross with these three women. Then, since we have such a limited amount of time, we need to put you in their path at every opportunity."

"Rita loves to paint early in the morning, and then again just before sunset. That would put her on the Boardwalk at those times," said Peter.

"Perfect for a romantic stroll at dusk along the beach," muttered Uncle Charlie, as he wrote furiously on the paper. He looked up and waved his hand, urging Peter to continue.

"The coffee shop is always busiest in the mornings, but they also make a nice lunch that fills the place up. Mac and I have stopped there for lunch a time or two before. "

Moira who interrupted Uncle Charlie's note-taking. "Well, the two of you need to be there for a late lunch, when it's quieter and the waitress can notice you more. Mackenzie, you need to dress romantically, not in your usual shorts and t-shirt. Let's make her imagination work and set the tone for romance."

Numbly, I nodded my head. I felt like things could get out of control very quickly. Moira and Uncle Charlie seemed to be enjoying this matchmaking game.

"And what about the General Store. How can we stand out in there?" I jumped in to ask.

"Mac, you're going to be very forgetful for the next couple days. And of course, me being the great friend that I am, I'll be willing to go with you in and out of the store to pick up the things that you keep forgetting. We must do a lot of flaunting the hand-holding and some quick little kisses in front of her."

Peter grinned at me, getting caught up in the game. My smile suddenly disappeared when I realized that this wasn't a game. He had to know this was serious, and every time we walked in front of one of these three women, we were upping the odds of something wrong happening. Something that could be dangerous and life-threatening to either Peter or myself. This wasn't the time to fool around.

"Mackenzie," Moira said, "it will be important that you and Peter act the same as you always do, except for being romantically involved. You can't let her, or anyone else, know what is going on because if they sense a trap—I fear what the outcome might be."

As much as I hated to admit it, Moira was right. I hadn't thought about that; one little mistake could make the difference between success and failure. And maybe life and death.

Uncle Charlie seemed satisfied with the rough plan and gave me a reassuring hug. It was a hug that I came to know over my years, and I was grateful for it.

"Well, I think we have an agenda. While you two are flaunting your romance in front of our suspects," Uncle Charlie began to chuckle at the word 'romance' but quickly covered it up with a cough, "I will do a little investigating on their backgrounds. Maybe if I drop a hint or two at Detective Byrd, we can have him working the other end of the investigation. He doesn't need to know how we've come up with these names, but I think if I approached it in the right way, he could consider them as well."

"Mackenzie, I think it's also important that you and I continue to work on your abilities to read the voices as you hear them,' Moira added. "I think I will shadow you, while you and Peter are acting out your little escapade. You can show me when you hear the voice, and I can be a second pair of eyes to look around and see who is in the area, and what their reactions are."

"But what about your job, Moira? Don't you have patients to see?"

She smiled as she thanked me for the concern. "That's not a big concern now, Mackenzie. I work as a consultant for the hospital, patient by patient. You were my last assigned case. I've been doing volunteer work while I wait for a new patient." Taking a breath, she continued, "This is how I found out about Isabella's murder. My time is my own, there are no obligations to stand in my way of taking a few days off.

"So, when do I begin with my new girlfriend?" Peter gave me a saucy wink and a light tickle at my side, as he asked the question. It was clear he was up for the challenge and was ready to jump right in and get working on finding out who the murderer was. For that matter, so was I. The sooner we can get this behind us, the better it would be. My uncle surprised me when he held his hands up as if putting a stop to our momentum.

"We want to make this as believable as possible, so let's not go jumping around all willy-nilly without being prepared. I think your first public appearance should be this evening. A quiet walk along the Boardwalk, in front of the artist, would be a perfect way to start. In the meantime, I'll start a few rumors about Mac's new boyfriend and how happy I am to see this young man become romantically involved with my niece. You all know just as well as I do how fast gossip spreads around here. By the time you go out on the beach, everybody will watch, wanting to know who Mac's new boyfriend is."

"That sounds like a splendid idea, Charlie. It will be much more credible if there's a rumor before they see something. Nothing encourages the imagination like a rumor. If we do this right, you'll be engaged by the time you walk the Boardwalk this evening," Moira chuckled.

Moira and Uncle Charlie seem pleased with themselves. Even Peter was nodding his head in agreement with their plan. Was I the only one who could see a disaster ahead of us? Or maybe I was just reading too much into it, letting my personal emotions take over when I should use common sense to catch a killer.

After the two men had gone, Moira turned to me. "I can tell you have deep feelings for Peter, Mackenzie. But, I don't think you need to worry, our activities will not jeopardize your friendship. Now, how about a bit of girl time? Let's go up and check out your wardrobe and see if we can find something that will make you look just a little more romantic. Maybe you have another skirt like that one you were to Ollie's, something in the wind could pick up and blow, so you create an alluring picture as you walk the pier with Peter. If you have one, I have the perfect peasant top with off the shoulders sleeves. I think with that, and maybe wear your hair down long, you'll create quite the vision. The more you look the part, the easier it will be to sell the concept of you and Peter being involved."

"Why not?" I said. "I may as well have fun with this. It looks like everybody else is going to enjoy the show."

"Don't fret so much, Mackenzie. Your uncle and Peter are very much aware of the risk in this plan. Their lightheartedness is a cover; we all need to be careful and watch out for the two of you. You ready? Let's head upstairs and see what we can come up with to enhance your beauty."

Deciding she was right, I got up and followed Moira up the stairs. Now that I wasn't so tense, I was looking forward to a little girl's time.

Chapter 20

I wasn't sure who Uncle Charlie talked to or what he said, but by four o'clock that afternoon, I already had two phone calls from friends wanting to find out if Peter and I were genuinely dating. The gossip mill had worked overtime today, and I applauded Uncle Charlie's decision.

By the time I took the third call, I could tell things were in motion. The last call came from Detective Byrd, asking if I remembered anything about the three suspects we had discussed. The little seeds of information my uncle had dropped on the detective's desk were working. Later, getting ready, I found myself feeling nervous as if this was a real first date. Excited too. Excited with the hope that something might come of it, and worried the opposite effect might happen and make our friendship awkward. That was the last thing I wanted to happen. I was finishing the final touches on my makeup, and I reached over and grabbed a hair-tie. Shaylee jumped up on the dresser and swiped the tie from my hand. I giggled at her. "Okay, missy, you win, I'll wear my hair down."

When Peter arrived to pick me up, he acted so natural that all my fears faded; it was just two friends having a good evening. His easy-going laugh put me at ease, as it always did, and he treated me the same as usual. At least he did until we got to the beach. Once he parked the car, he became courtly and put on the show of wooing me. He rushed to my side of the car, holding the door open for me, and once I stood next to him, he reached out and held my hand. At first, this made me a little jumpy, but then he brought my hand to his lips and gave it a kiss and a wink at the same time; the show had begun. As we made our way to the Boardwalk, it appeared everyone else in town had the same idea. We said hello to friends as we passed them, and a few comments were made about the hand-holding from Peter's friends, but nobody seemed to think it out of place. I looked around, wondering where my second set of eyes could be. Then I noticed Moira walking towards us from the other end of the Boardwalk with someone. As we got closer, I realized she was with Uncle Charlie, who held her arm in an old-fashioned way. They appeared natural together as if they had known each other for years. Secretly, I thought Uncle Charlie needed friends and Moira was a perfect solution.

We greeted each other as if it had been days, instead of hours, since we'd seen each other. And that was the image we wanted to portray. Everything needed to be causal, from our meeting Moira and Charlie to my hand clasped firmly in Peter's. The laughter was genuine, and others walking by stopped to say hi. It didn't seem all that different from any other evening. But it was, and I knew it. Beneath the laughter, I was tense, like a small child caught doing something wrong, waiting for her punishment.

Even though I took part in the surrounding conversation, I was also fully aware of every person who walked past us, whether they spoke to me or not. I tried hard to remember the instructions Moira had given me about developing a deeper awareness of the things going on around me. A few times, I picked up on an underlining tension from someone, but it was fleeting, and I couldn't honestly say I had really noticed anything different. I sighed in frustration, and Peter squeezed my hand for courage. I felt better knowing I wasn't on my own in this scheme; the man holding my hand made it clear that I had his protection if needed.

Uncle Charlie turned to Moira and suggested they continue their walk.

"You two go enjoy yourselves, and we'll catch up later. There is a wonderful artist down the Boardwalk, you should stop by and see her work," Uncle Charlie suggested, setting us up with a purpose to leave and head in Gloria's direction.

"I love her work," I responded gaily, amazed at myself for being such a good actress. "Uncle Charlie's right, let's go see what she's working on tonight."

Moira blew us a kiss, and Uncle Charlie winked before they headed in the opposite direction. I inwardly groaned, the two of them seemed to be enjoying this more than necessary. But on the lighter side of things, they did look good together.

Peter tugged on my hand, pulling me out of my thoughts and back to the present. Strolling down the Boardwalk, Peter put his arm over my shoulder with casual ease as we walked. It seemed so natural, and Peter's body so close to mine felt comfortable, and I felt we were meant to be together like this. I caught him looking at me thoughtfully a couple of times as we walked. I hoped they were positive thoughts.

When we approached the artist, a small crowd had gathered around her easel as people watched her paint the setting sun. There was no denying her talent, and I had stopped a few times before to watch her work. I even had one of her paintings hanging in the guest room. It always amazed me how she could talk as she painted. She carried on complete conversations with anybody who would stop by, answering questions about her painting or exchanging idle gossip and chitchat with locals.

Gloria smiled in greeting when she looked up from her canvas and recognized us. As we joined in the conversation, Peter leaned against the rail of the Boardwalk and pulled me in front of him, wrapping his arms around me, resting his chin on the back of my head. The movement was so smooth, it seemed natural for the two of us to stand there like that.

There were a few raised eyebrows from the others around us when they realized the rumors were true. Peter was making it obvious we were a couple. I noticed Gloria tilt her head as if questioning what she saw as she looked in our direction.

"Gloria, that's beautiful. I don't know how you make each painting look different. But they're all spectacular. I love the one I have at my house; when I look at it, I can almost feel the wetness from the waves."

I was sincere with my compliment, but I also wanted to start a conversation with the woman. I needed to hear her voice, I needed to hear if there was any anger or resentment when she talked.

Before she had a chance to answer, a few other people chimed in adding their compliments about her paintings, and it took a few moments before she answered me.

"Thank you so much, Mac. All artists want to know their work is appreciated. Everyone asks me how I can do so many paintings of the same scenery. I don't see it as the same scenery; the ocean is ever-changing with no two waves hitting the beach the same, no sunset matches the previous one. It's simply a matter of looking for what catches my eye at that moment and expanding on it to create the painting. It's not an exact science, but it works for me." She laughed as she gave her explanation, trying to put into words how she felt about her painting.

I heard the passion in her voice, and maybe a bit of wistfulness. But there was no anger, no resentment, and no hatred. Gloria's was not the voice that echoed in my head, and no matter how much imagination I used, there was no connecting the words spoken with such emotion with the woman in front of me.

I think Peter could sense my frustration through my trembling hands and gave me a slight squeeze of encouragement. "She's only the first one, Mac. Two more to go, don't give up," Peter whispered in my ear.

Since Gloria had been our only goal for the evening, I relaxed. No sense in letting a perfectly good sunset go to waste. And there was nothing more to do tonight. Before long, the conversation between some in the gathering around Gloria turned from painting to fishing. I listened for a few moments, but I'd heard most of these stories before, and like most fish stories, they got bigger and more exaggerated each time told. It didn't take long for me to tune out the surrounding voices. Instead, I thought about the arms holding me. I wondered how it would be to be held in his arms for real, not just as a show. Feeling like it was natural, I snuggled closer against Peter's chest, content as his arms tightened with my movement.

When the sun finally set, making it too dark for Gloria to continue painting, she packed up her supplies. Then she reached into a basket she had at her side, pulled out a bottle of wine and paper cups. I had heard that this was her ritual at the end of an evening, and she was more than willing to share wine with her admirers. As the fish stories grew, so did the laughter. It didn't take long before others joined in. This wasn't an uncommon way for us to spend an evening on the beach. In our small town, we welcomed anyone who joined us on the Boardwalk.

I had completely forgotten the reason we were there, I was enjoying the company so much. Because of this, I was unprepared when a sharp pain in my ankle took my breath away before I heard the voice.

"So, the rumors are true. Peter, what have you done? When will you noticed me?"

I jerked away from Peter in a panic and looked around, but I could see nothing in the darkness. I tried to concentrate and remember all that Moira told me, but it was too late, the woman seemed to be walking away from us. The sharp pain in my ankle had changed to mild irritation.

Peter knew instinctively what had happened and, making excuses, he told the others we were leaving. Grabbing my hand, he started to lead me back up the Boardwalk, in the direction we had come. I knew this could be a mistake; we were heading into a dark area, and we would be alone. In a quick decision, I invited three of the guys that Peter and I often paddle-boarded with to join us for pizza at my place. They agreed without a second thought, and I nodded to myself; they would be perfect reinforcements for our safety home. Peter gave me a slight nod, acknowledging that he realized what I was doing, and then the five of us headed back to my place laughing as if nothing was out of place.

Chapter 21

I woke up with a start and an awful crick in my neck. It seemed I never made it up to my bedroom the night before, falling asleep on the couch instead, and I was paying for it now. I rubbed my eyes and saw Shaylee staring down at me from the back of the couch. It was clear she thought this was an unusual circumstance and was wondering what was going on with me. I pulled myself up into a sitting position, untangling my legs from the comforter as I did and patted my lap. I petted Shaylee for a few moments, and after mutual admiration for each other, she meowed and jumped down, heading to the kitchen. It was clear to see where her priorities were, and that was breakfast.

"Okay, okay, I'm coming, you're not going to starve," I reassured the cat as I got up to follow her.

It wasn't a graceful movement as I tripped over my own shoes. I groaned to myself as I remembered the night before and the hungry guests that had joined Peter and me for pizza. Between the five of us, we had gone through three trays of pizza, and since I only had two slices, that left the rest for the guys. The groan was because I could remember everything being dumped in my kitchen before they had left; there was still a mess in there needing to be cleaned.

Throughout the evening, and in the presence of his best buds, Peter kept up the pretense of being in a relationship with me. He sat close to me and held my hand, when he wasn't picking up another piece of pizza. And the laughter and rowdiness of the night before had kept my fears at bay. There was no way another voice would be noticed, not even in my head, with all the laughter. Whoever the woman was, she was drowned out. The guys stayed until late and Peter left with them, at my insistence. I remember locking up after they had left and collapsing on the couch, exhausted, and that was the last thing I remembered until I opened my eyes to see my pretty little kitty staring at me, waiting for her breakfast.

After feeding the cat and putting my kitchen back to order, I poured myself a cup of coffee and made my way to my office. There, sitting in the middle of my desk, was the piece of rock the two lifeguards had given me. I remember Peter had picked it up from the coffee table in the living room when things got a little rowdy last night and moved it to my office for safety. When he picked it up, the guys talked about how these rocks were formed, and then they carefully examined the "coolest scar ever" on my ankle.

I walked across the room and picked it up from my desk, intending to move it back to the living room. As soon as I touched it, I had a clear remembrance of that tone of voice from last night, and shivers ran up and down my spine. Not wanting to dwell on it now while I was by myself, I hurriedly took it out and put it back in its location where it belonged.

I worked until the need for a fresh cup of coffee made itself known. Putting away the paperwork, I went into the kitchen and downed half a cup before a car pulled into the driveway. Peter knocked on the door and opened it in the same motion, the type of forwardness only a good friend would take. He had a cheerful smile on his face, full of energy, ready to face the new challenges. After tousling my hair in greeting, he headed straight to the coffee pot.

"Hope you slept okay, Mac, we were here pretty late. So, before the others get here, what do you think? Is Gloria our primary suspect, or do we keep looking?"

I thought about what he said as I held my hand out for him to refill my cup too. Like an old married couple, words were unnecessary, and Peter automatically filled it and handed me a packet of sweetener while he pushed my favorite flavored creamer in my direction.

"I don't know, Peter. Gloria seems so open and unencumbered with anything. She's such a free spirit, I can't imagine her pining over somebody to the point of obsessing. And let's face it, she's a beautiful woman. If she wanted you, she would simply tell you and shrug her shoulders if you turned her down." I hesitated for a second, feeling slight jealously thinking she'd want Peter, but refocused quickly. "And it wasn't her voice I heard, and I don't think even under duress I could stretch my imagination to make it her voice."

Taking a sip of his coffee, Peter agreed with me. "Yeah, that's kind of what I was thinking too."

We sat down at the table, and Peter grabbed the pad that had the three names circled on it. Grabbing a pen, he crossed off Gloria's name with a flourish.

"Well, that takes care of one, only two more to go. Who do you think we should investigate first?" he asked, holding a make-believe pipe as if he was Sherlock Holmes. I had to laugh out loud at his shenanigans.

"I figured we would talk to Uncle Charlie and Moira first before we decide. They might have a few thoughts, or maybe they saw something we didn't see last night. Rather than walking into a situation blindly, I want to make sure we are taking all the precautions we can. Like last night, having the guys come home with us."

"I have to admit Mac, that was a pretty smart move inviting those three to join us. I never even gave it a thought about us walking home alone in the dark. We definitely would've been easy pickings for someone with murderous intent."

"Thanks, it sure didn't hurt their feelings to be offered an extra meal of pizza. Where do you guys put all that food?"

He joined my laughter and made a comment about growing boys. With a wink, I held my hands out wide at my sides and warned him that that type of consumption could easily lead to the wrong kind of growth. We were still chuckling when Uncle Charlie came in through the front door, yelling out a good morning.

Giving me a kiss on the forehead as he walked by, he grabbed a cup out of the cupboard and poured himself a cup of coffee. After his first sip, he gave a sigh of contentment.

"I don't know what it is about your coffee, Mac, but it always tastes good. By the way, I passed Moira on my way, she should be here in a couple minutes, and we all need to sit down and go over last night's events. I can't stay long—I need to be in court in a few hours, but I wanted to make sure we all touched base before I left for the day." Uncle Charley's words brought everything back into focus, reminding me what our priorities needed to be: find out who Isabella's killer was.

Taking another sip from his cup, Uncle Charlie walked over to the table and sat down, straightening his shoulders as if he was getting ready for a deposition. His stance was familiar: it meant it was all business mode, with no room for fun and games. I remembered from experience on days he had to appear in court, that's how he started his mornings out, and he never broke from that mode until he finished for the day. And maybe that's what we needed; someone to hold us on target and get to work. Somehow, I was positive there was little time to be lost. The woman whose voice I kept hearing was sounding more angry and volatile, and I remembered the old saying about a woman scorned.

"Mac, you may as well make a pot of tea for Moira. She's not a coffee drinker. By the time it's ready, she should be here, and we can scope out a plan for the two of you to follow today."

I nodded my head in agreement, wondering how he knew she was a tea drinker, and got out my favorite teapot and the brand of tea Moira likes. By the time I finished brewing Moira's pot of tea, she was walking through the back door, a statement about how fast of friends we had become. After greeting everyone and pouring herself her first cup of tea, we were all sitting around the table, throwing out ideas. After a few moments of discussion, we came to the agreement that taking a late coffee break would be the perfect excuse to go to the coffee shop and question our next suspect. We thought if we went in late, there wouldn't be as many people, and we could concentrate on what was going on with our suspect. I needed to watch how she reacted to seeing Peter and I enter as a couple.

Now that we had all agreed on what the next move was, it was time for me to tell them about the voice from last night, and what she had said.

"I was pretty sure something happened before we left. That's the real reason you asked the guys to come home with us, isn't it?"

"Yes, I was going to say something to you last night, but there was no opportunity."

"Well, based on her referencing the rumor, we can determine that she is someone local. Someone that would be part of or close enough to overhear what is going on in the gossip mill." Uncle Charlie seemed to think out loud, not expecting an answer.

"She is very obsessed with you, Peter. And she seems to think you should have the same feelings for her," I glanced at Peter, hoping he would understand the warning in my voice. "Each time she speaks, we have more information and are better able to protect each other. Now we simply must go ahead with our plans and see what happens."

Satisfied that we had an agenda for our day, Uncle Charlie pushed back his chair and got up to leave. He surprised me by asking Peter to walk him to the front door. As they left the room, Moira looked at me with a question clear in her eyes, but I shrugged my shoulders. I know my Uncle Charlie well, and I figured he was probably giving Peter advice and insisting he looked out for me. What Uncle Charlie didn't understand was I would be looking out for Peter. Or maybe he understood we had each other's backs. Just like always—we've had each other's back since we were kids. A few minutes later, Peter returned to the kitchen, a grin on his face.

"Your uncle gave me some good advice, Mac. He suggested we go nowhere alone. Since I agree, I'm sticking around here. If it's ok with you, I'm going to go use your office and check my emails and make some phone calls before we head out for our coffee date."

After Peter went into the office, Moira, Shaylee, and I headed out to the garden. Shaylee saw us walking towards the door, she was ahead of us waiting to be let out. The garden has undoubtedly become her private domain and she always seems to want to be out ahead of me whenever I entered the garden. If I didn't know better, I would say she was doing guard patrol before I walked out.

I've always felt at peace here. I must admit, since my incident with the lightning, I've been even more content in my garden than ever before. I found myself being lulled into a catatonic state, drifting off almost into a daze. Sometimes I've sat on my swing watching the butterflies and dragonflies drift back and forth. If I stared hard enough, I could imagine them becoming something otherworldly, but something always seemed to distract me when I got to this stage. Usually, it was Shaylee swatting at the same dragonfly I'm watching, almost as if she was shooing it away.

That morning the garden seemed to have a more magical feeling to it, and I attributed it to the fact that the gardenias were in full bloom. I could even smell the mint growing. It was still early enough that the heat hadn't gotten to the garden and it was pleasant to sit and enjoy the natural aroma-therapy my herbs created.

Moira and I sat in the swing, we didn't say much, both content and concentrating on our own thoughts. Before long, Peter was standing at the door, calling out to say it was almost time to head into town. When we ambled back into the house, I wasn't surprised to see that Peter had made himself a sandwich. Laughing, I shook my head at him.

"You realize the idea of going to a coffee shop is to get something more than coffee. If we're going to draw attention to ourselves, we'll need to order something to eat."

"And your point is?" Peter chuckled and took a bite into the sandwich. "This is just a snack to tide me over before we have a real meal. Go grab your purse, or whatever else you need, and let's head to the coffee shop where I can show off my best girl." Throwing his arms around my shoulders, Peter gave me a hug and then pushed me in the direction towards my room. Oh, how I wished his words were true, but somehow, I was sure this was still a bit of a game to him. One I hope he wouldn't lose.

Chapter 22

We made it to the cafe with perfect timing, arriving in between the breakfast and lunch rush-hour patrons. The cafe was almost empty, but there were still patrons lingering or, like us, wandering in to catch a mid-morning coffee. We were the center of attention by being the only new patrons and we watched to determine the reaction of the barista when she saw the two of us together as a couple. It was as if a director was bringing his cast on stage for the second act of a play. Everything was in place, and the stage was set to draw out our suspect.

The coffee shop was just like any other coffee shop in a small town, proudly taking a prime piece of real estate on Main Street, with large windows overlooking the sidewalk. The passing pedestrians could glance in and see who was goofing off for the morning. Often somebody rushing by would see a friend inside and stop to join them. It was a constant ebb and flow of customers coming and going and it seemed to be the hot spot of town for catching up on the latest gossip.

Since we wanted to be sure to be the center of attention, we took the main table by the front window. I figured this way, even if we had the wrong suspect, at least we had a chance of more people seeing us as they walked by, enjoying those last few days of summer freedom before vacations ended, and jobs and classes called them back into their daily routines. It wouldn't take long for word to get out that Peter and I were a couple.

When Judy's name had shown up on the list of possible suspects, it surprised me. Judy was a true introvert, and how she ever came to work in the coffee shop, around so many people, is something I couldn't figure out. It was almost painful to watch her try to interact with strangers. She didn't seem to loosen up with people she'd known for a while either. I would often go out of my way to include her in a conversation, but it always seemed to falter, and I would walk away feeling sad for her. I had noticed that she seemed to be at ease with the elderly customers and she could chit-chat with them easily.

Peter and I were talking to mutual friends when Judy came to the table to take our order. She waited patiently for us to realize she was there and gave me a shy smile when I told her I was sorry she had to wait for us.

"That's okay, Mac. I can wait until you're ready."

She moved away, but Peter stopped her with his friendly smile.

"We're ready now, Judy. How have you been? Looks like the morning rush is finished. Guess that means you won't mind if Mac and I hang out here for a bit." Reaching across the table, Peter grabbed my hand and kissed it on the palm side. It felt like a lover's kiss, not a best friend's kiss, and I gave a little shiver. But there was no time to think about it any further, as I wanted to observe Judy's reaction to Peter's movements.

She averted her eyes, and a slight blush spread across her cheeks. I saw she was uncomfortable with the open display of affection, but I didn't discern any other deep emotions. I smiled at her, hoping to put her at ease and asked what the coffee of the day was.

"It's a strong Colombian mix. Everyone seems to enjoy it."

"That sounds perfect, and strong coffee will chase away the mid-morning dull-drums. How about two cups and a Danish for each of us? How is the Wi-Fi speed today?"

It was a running joke that you could never tell what type of reception the Internet service would offer from day to day in the coffee shop, a bone of contention for the owners, who were trying to create a Starbuck's atmosphere.

"It's a little touchy today. That might be why we're so empty right now. No one is staying to work online," Judy answered my question with a wry grin.

"Then, no one else will need our table. Perfect. We can spend quiet time together, Mac." Peter pushed the issue of our spending time together as Judy wrote down our order.

The young woman said nothing more, only nodding her head in agreement. Putting her pen behind her ear in a long-practiced movement, she left our table to get our order together. I saw her reflection in the window and noticed she was watching us intently while she poured the coffee. I don't know if it was because we were one of the few customers she had now or if she was trying to comprehend our new relationship status. But I read nothing negative from her. And her voice was nothing like the one I kept hearing in my head. I had my doubts that Judy Nick was the killer.

As soon as Judy was out of hearing range, Peter looked over at me, seeming to be a tad worried.

"I don't know, Mac. It's awful hard to cast her as a jealous woman with a murderous temperament. What if Melissa is a bust too? We'll be out of suspects."

"Hey, don't jump ahead of yourself. And even if these three don't pan out, then we start over. Even if we need to walk the streets until I hear the voice again. I'm not giving up, Peter."

"Yeah, you're right. We've just started. Maybe we'll get lucky and you'll hear the voice soon and you'll be able to tell who it belongs too."

"Lucky? I'm not sure I want that kind of luck. I just want this to be over, so I can get back to normal."

Peter squeezed my hand and gently held it until Judy returned with our order. I caught Judy staring at our hands, but she said nothing. Giving us a small, shy smile, she returned to cleaning tables.

"Try your Danish," Peter said as he took a bite, "it's fantastic."

He chuckled as I wiped a dab of cream cheese from the corner of his mouth,

"Yes, I can see that," I tried to keep a straight face but ended up giggling when Peter made a face at me.

After taking a bite of mine, I turned somber. I should be concentrating on the surrounding atmosphere, searching for the sign we were on the right path. But it was no use. There was nothing out of the ordinary for me to pick up on, not here. With a sigh, I took a swallow of my coffee and wondered what would happen next.

Chapter 23

Peter and I lingered over our coffee as long as possible, but finally, we realized we needed to leave before we made Judy suspicious. We had stretched out our time talking to the few patrons who had wandered in to order a cup to go. I had even tried to speak to Judy, but she answered in her usual one-line way. She either didn't want to talk to me, or she really was as shy as I thought. When she answered, her voice was soft, almost girlish, and I felt confident she wasn't the person we were looking to find.

The time spent lingering over our coffee wasn't a total waste. Peter and I had a serious talk about his job and how he felt he was getting nowhere within the company. I was happy to be his sounding board and offered suggestions. Peter had earned his degree in finance, under his parent's urging, with the goal for him to someday take over his father's firm. I had known for a long time that he wasn't happy at his job, and he was beginning to figure out for himself that he needed to follow his own path for his future. He was interested in law but hadn't figured out what part of the law he wanted to consider.

"Peter, you worry too much. Your parents will support you, no matter what you do. The only way you could possibly disappoint them is to go in a direction that will make you miserable. The degree you have in finance will never go to waste, and you probably only need to take a few extra classes once you decide on a path."

"You're probably right, but I feel like I'm letting my dad down."

"That's nonsense-and they would be upset to hear you talking like this. Trust me."

"Mac, my parents have always had a special spot for you. Maybe if you talked to them…"

"Sorry, Peter, this has to come from you. Give them a chance to hear you out. I think you'll be surprised." Picking up my empty cup, I looked inside, not remembering when I had finished it. I glanced over towards Judy but seeing her glance at the clock over the counter and frown, I didn't dare ask for another refill.

"We're wearing out our welcome, Peter. It might be a good idea to leave now before we get kicked out."

Peter looked at his watch. He was as surprised as I was to find we'd been sitting there for almost an hour and a half. He put a large tip on the table, to make up for our holding up a table for so long, and then came around behind me to pull my chair out for me. Leaning over, he gave me a quick kiss on the check.

"See, Mom raised me with some old-fashioned manners," he teased.

"She would be proud to see you using them, too." I teased back. Then I called out a goodbye to Judy as we moved towards the exit. She gave a weak wave in response and moved in to clear our table.

Once outside, we stood on the sidewalk, looking at each other. Before either of us said a word, my cell phone rang. I saw the call was from Uncle Charlie and I quickly answered.

"I don't have a lot of time, Mac. I need to get back into the judge's chambers to discuss a fine point of injustice. But, I thought you might need an excuse to go to the general store, and since I need a few things, I thought you and Peter could pick them up for me. Oh, dinner is at my place, Moira will be meeting us there around four."

"I could have made up an excuse, Uncle Charlie."

"Oh, I'm sure you could, but this way, you can help me too."

I laughed at my uncle, he was always thinking ahead. Agreeing with his plan, I asked what he needed, repeating the items out loud for Peter to help me remember them. As I hung up, I realized that this had been Uncle Charlie's way of checking up on me. He wouldn't come out and say he was worried, but I read the signs. And I loved him even more for it. He took his role of guardianship seriously, a promise made to my parents long before they had ever imagined it would be necessary.

"Well, it looks like we need to head over to the general store. I'm not holding my breath on Melissa being our murderess, either. Not unless she were to bury you under all that ice cream."

"Wow, what a way to go!" joked Peter as he took my hand and started down the sidewalk in the store's direction.

My doubts about Melissa were strong. Yet if it wasn't her, and we had just ruled out the other two, then what? The murderer might be anyone in town. Even one of our friends. I hated that thought and quickly dismissed it. Before I took a step, Peter grabbed my hand and pulled me to a stop.

"How about if we take a detour? All that talking we did about my job has me thinking, and I'd like to just walk for a bit. Do you mind?"

"Not a problem at all, I'm all yours. Which way, the beach or the park?"

He grinned at me. "What do you think, little knucklehead?" He pulled me in the direction of the waterfront, just as I figured he would. My mind was screaming that our world was dangerous, yet it was also swooning over Peter's joke with me. I missed that part of us. Hopefully, we can get back to the subject of us and where we're going in our future before too long. I was beginning to enjoy his arms around me and his eyes only for me.

After we had walked up and down the sandy shore line for a while, holding hands, skipping rocks, and enjoying the early afternoon breeze, he stopped and pulled me toward him.

"Mac, I'm invited to Charlie's for dinner, too, right?"

I looked into his eyes and saw that they were hooded as if he wanted to keep from showing his true feelings. I then looked at his mouth, and I yearned to be kissed. I took a deep breath to clear my head. I knew the timing wasn't right yet. *Stay in focus*, I told myself.

Peter continued his thought, not knowing what was going through my mind. "I'll try to talk to him after we eat. He'll have some good advice for me. I'm almost ready to make the decision about venturing into the field of law, and I'm leaning towards investigative work. I know he has plenty of connections here in town I might use. This will work out great, Mac. Guess we'd better head over to Melissa's shop and pick up the items he needs. And pay attention to Melissa while we are there. Ready to go play the lovesick couple?"

I returned his smile and nodded. He looked so handsome, with his thick hair spiking all over the place as the wind played with it, and his deep blue eyes looking shiny again. He wasn't only handsome, but he looked taller than his six-foot-two frame as if a great weight had been lifted from his strong shoulders. If only I could tell him I wasn't playing the part of a lovesick woman. Slipping my arm through his, I bat my eyelashes.

"Lead the way, sweetheart," I gushed playfully.

Peter had a knack for taking mundane, everyday items and twisting them until you're laughing hysterically. He waved to two kids walking their dog, and soon his comments about the kids and their dog were becoming outrageous. The simple act of dog walking had turned into a wild adventure, as Peter told his story of all the trouble the dog had gotten the two kids into. I didn't know if it was ever possible for two boys and one dog to get into as much trouble as Peter was portraying, but he had me laughing until the tears ran down my cheeks.

Our laughter brought smiles to the customers in the store as we walked inside, and I was surprised how busy the store was at that time of day. Melissa was behind the ice cream counter, as usual, trying to help a youngster decide what flavor of ice cream she wanted for her second scoop on her waffle cone. Peter and I wandered around the store, hoping to catch Melissa after the crowd had thinned out. I needed to get her to talk, to judge both her voice and her tone, but I wouldn't get a clear picture of that with other people milling around.

I grabbed a handbasket and started to pick up the items Uncle Charlie had asked for.

Finally, the youngster made her major decision and left, a happy camper. Melissa greeted us warmly as we walked over to counter.

"So, I see the rumors are true. It's about time you two became a couple. I mean, you've been coming here together since you were both knee-high to a grasshopper. Remember that time Peter's braces got stuck to the sleeve of your sweater?" She laughed hardily, showing her teeth. We couldn't help laughing with her. "How about a hot fudge sundae to celebrate?"

While Melissa prepared the two hot fudge sundaes, Peter kept her in conversation. That allowed me to listen to her voice and see if I could hear anything that remotely resembled what I have heard in my head. But Melissa's voice sounded nothing at all like the one that was haunting me.

I was frustrated and wondered what we were going to do. It was apparent none of the three women we had suspected could be Isabella's killer. While Melissa was talking to Peter, I wondered if Detective Byrd had any luck on his end of the investigation and how willing he would be to tell me. I knew quite a few members of the police force through my uncle, and I wondered if I could call in some favors. In my mind, I went through the contacts I had with some of the policemen, trying to decide who would be the most cooperative and willing to go behind detective Byrd's back and give us information.

After Melissa handed us our ice cream, Peter swiftly grabbed the cherry off the top of mine. I playfully swatted at him because he's been doing this for I don't even know how long. He knew darn well I wanted it.

It was Melissa who gave me a push in the right direction on who to contact when she began talking about a grant I had been working on for the community.

"Mac, I can't tell you enough how much the Youth-Works Center appreciates all the work you're doing for them. My sister was so pleased with the first part of the grant they received and the good it's accomplishing already. I know for a fact it's keeping a few of those little ruffians off the street and putting them into an environment where they've been learning respect and accountability for themselves."

Melissa's sister worked in the police department with the troubled youth of the town, trying to keep them on the straight and narrow. I had been working on getting grants to provide tutoring and research projects for them at the Environmental Learning Center, hoping that with something interesting added to their lives, we could point them in positive directions.

I suddenly had a thought. She not only worked with the youth, but she was also on staff at the police department and would be the perfect person to get us the information we were looking for. I thought she would do it, not only because I'd worked so hard for her on the grants, but because she would want to see justice done just as much as we did.

"Hey, how is Diana? She wouldn't happen to be working today, would she?"

"Yeah, she is. She was complaining last night that she had the afternoon shift today. I'm sure she would love for you to stop by, so she could thank you herself."

Smiling back at Melissa, I lifted a spoonful of ice cream and hot fudge, ready to put it in my mouth.

"I just might do that. Peter, would you like to take a walk with me down to the station after you finish your ice cream?" I held my ice cream bowl above my head, trying to keep it away from Peter, who was gesturing with his spoon trying to get at it. "I have a feeling you'll be eating half of mine, too."

We laughed at Peter's obvious enjoyment of eating ice cream. Some boys never grew up.

Chapter 24

After we left Melissa's with Uncle Charlie's items in tow, we headed to the business district where the police headquarters sat. We asked for Diana and were told to wait in the lobby. It was obvious that the summer's slow pace had reached even here. I could hear the murmur of voices from behind the desk, but we were the only ones in the waiting area. I gave a shiver of discomfort, but I wasn't sure if it was from the uneasy feeling of being in the station or the fact they had the air conditioner set so low.

Diana came out to greet us, and I noticed she had a sweater on. It gave me a sense of relief to realize it wasn't only me who was shivering. I could never understand why public buildings must be kept so cold unless it was to encourage you to take care of your business and leave.

"Mac, what a welcome surprise," Diana said as she came out and hugged me. "I've meant to call you. Peter, it's nice to see you again. Why don't the two of you come on back to my office? I've got some great pictures of the kids to share with you, Mac. I can't tell you how much that grant has provided for our program."

Peter and I followed her past the reception desk and down a narrow hallway to her office. While we were trying to find a soft spot in the worn-out chairs, she rummaged through the top desk drawer and pulled out an envelope.

I was thrilled to find the practical use they were making of the grant. And I could tell it was being used properly, from the smiles on the children's faces. I had met those kids, and it was rare for some of them to crack a smile. But I saw outright laughter and joy, and it made my job so worthwhile. Every line I filled out, every form I signed, was what it was all about: the kids.

We talked for a few moments about the photos, and Diana regaled us with a few stories of the more interesting episodes with the kids. After placing the envelope back in her desk drawer, she asked, "So, you didn't come down here to talk about the kids, did you, Mac? I could have emailed you the pictures. What's up?"

"I admit, I have an ulterior reason." I cleared my throat in nervousness. "I was hoping you could help us, but I don't want to put your job in jeopardy and have you stepping on any toes on our behalf."

"Well, out with it, Mac. If it's something I can't do, I'll let you know. You're not going to ask me to hide a crime for you, are you?"

I gave a weak laugh.

"Oh, no. Just the opposite. I'm, or rather we, are trying to find out information about the progress of an on-going investigation. Normally, I would never consider putting my nose where it doesn't belong, but we're somewhat involved." I gauged her reaction. I didn't notice an immediate rejection, so I continued.

"A mutual friend of ours was murdered. We were with her earlier the night it happened, and, to tell the truth, we're anxious to find out if there's been any progress or new leads."

"Ah, Isabella Rossi. I can understand why you'd be anxious. Nasty case. She was a friend of yours?"

"Hmmm," I gave a quick glance at Peter before I continued, "more Peter's than mine. I had just met her. But I liked her, and I can't help wondering if it could have been one of us murdered instead of Isabella. It seems so unlikely for anyone around here to be a victim of murder."

Getting up out of her chair, Diana walked over to her office door and poked her head out. She looked up and down the hallway before she closed the door.

"Okay, this isn't for public knowledge, and I'll deny that I said anything to you if I get questioned. Are we clear?" Waiting until we both nodded in agreement, she leaned across the papers piled in the center of her desk. Peter and I both leaned forward in our chairs, eager to hear what she had to say. She dropped her voice to a conspiratorial level.

"Detective Byrd is pulling his hair out on this case. It seems all his clues are dead ends." Her head nodded towards Peter. "I hate to say it, Peter, but I think he was pinning his hope on you being a murderer. Mac, when you provided a solid alibi for Peter, it really put a hole in this case. I know there've been a few leads coming in, but they don't seem to lead anywhere. We do know that whoever did this was mad with anger." She paused there as if she were about to give us some bad news. "I hate to leak the gory details, but the victim was bludgeoned so badly it was hard to identify her. That came from some seriously pent up anger." Diana hesitated, her brow wrinkled and then pointed a finger at me, making her point clear.

"You're not getting involved in this, are you two? This is not the time to play Nancy Drew and one of the Hardy Boys. I would hate for either one of you to get hurt."

Peter and I glanced at each other.

"It's okay Mac, tell her," Peter said as he touched my arm in reassurance.

"Well, we are involved. Like you said, everything pointed to Peter, plus she was a friend of his. It's awful knowing we were the last people to see her before her death and that we couldn't do anything to prevent it."

Diana glanced at the closed office door before she continued. "I can tell you that the three suspects your Uncle Charlie pointed out to Detective Byrd are being thoroughly investigated. Of course, doing a proper job means considering their backgrounds, and that can take time. In the meantime, we'll just keep asking questions and re-interviewing anyone who was with her within twenty-four hours from the time of her death. I understand it was quite crowded at Ollie's that night, and we haven't gone through the entire witness interrogation yet. Then we must decipher through fact and fiction. You know, as well as I do, after a couple of drinks in a dim bar, what you see may not be what you really see."

"You're right, it was crowded that night. You must have a pretty big list of potential witnesses to go through, right? Have they given you any other possible leads?"

"Peter, I can't answer that, not without jeopardizing both my job and the investigation. If Detective Byrd knew you were in here asking questions, he'd be furious."

We were working circles around each other, and there would be no more valuable information coming out of Diana. But her comment about the crowded bar made me pause. I was close enough to Peter that I could give him a little nudge with my shoe. He caught on, and within moments, we were saying our goodbyes.

As we were leaving, we, unfortunately, met up with Detective Byrd, who was walking by. At first, he seemed as if he would keep walking, but he turned back to us.

He glared pointedly at Peter, and then he turned to me and gave me a stern look as well.

"I'm surprised to find the two of you here. Did you remember something else about the murder that you forgot to tell me? Something that might be of use to the investigation?"

After squirming under his intense look for a moment, I glanced at the black plastic clock hanging on the far wall. I turned to Peter. "We need to go if we want to make it to Uncle Charlie's on time," I said, hoping he'd catch the hint that I wanted to get away from this detective as soon as possible.

At the mention of my uncle's name, Detective Byrd had one last parting comment. "You can let your uncle know I've placed surveillance on a few of his potential suspects. Not that it's doing any good. But I wouldn't want him to think I was ignoring his suggestions. You can also tell him the mayor is looking forward to a round of golf at the club. Of course, I'll be out working those leads and won't be able to join those who can find the time for such leisurely pursuits."

There was a self-pity tone to his voice, mixed with more than a touch of sarcasm. I could understand his frustration and bit my lip to keep from making a snappy retort.

Chapter 25

We laughed like two kids who had gotten away with something as we stood on the front steps of the police station. Still grinning at each other, we heard somebody call out. Turning, we saw Roger walking in our direction.

He gave me a warm hello before turning to Peter. "Hey, can we talk for a second?"

"Sure, Rog. Hon, excuse us for a sec."

My heart fluttered. No, not because of an angry voice inside my head, but because I had just heard Peter call me 'hon.' I had no time to analyze it, but now I was more determined than ever to get this behind us so that we can discuss our possible future together.

When I glanced over to the guys, I saw Roger handing Peter a folded piece of tin foil and Peter handing him some money. I swear if I hadn't known Peter any better, this would have looked like a drug deal. And right outside the police station! Peter looked up and noticed me watching him, and he gave me a smile and a wink, so I let it go and wouldn't bother asking him about what I'd seen. I figured if he wanted to tell me he would.

Uncle Charlie had a beautiful home, only minutes from the police station. Located on a side street, lined with large Live Oaks, we walked in the shade, and we enjoyed the rest of the way in relative coolness. I was surprised to find that Moira was already there. She and Uncle Charlie sat on the front porch, chatting and enjoying a glass of iced tea. I was thrilled to see Uncle Charlie sitting in the company of such a beautiful and kind-hearted woman, with a smile on his face. Too often, his only company were his clients, and believe me, there weren't that many smiles when they were going over their cases.

"Come on up and join us, there's plenty for everyone. We're both dying to hear how you made out this morning. We may as well sit here and talk, I've already arranged for dinner to be delivered in a couple hours."

As Peter and I joined them, I leaned over and gave Uncle Charlie a kiss on the cheek to reassure him that I was fine. Moira poured two large glasses of iced tea, handing one to each of us as we sat down.

We spent the next half-hour re-hashing the morning's events. Everything was re-hashed repeatedly in minute detail until my head began to pound. We talked in circles about everything that had happened, and in the process, we discussed each suspect and their reaction.

"Are you sure you didn't miss anything? Between the two of you, did you carefully watch their reactions?" Uncle Charlie asked as he grilled us one last time.

"We both watched everything and we made sure we acted flamboyantly with our affection for each other. There's no way anyone could have misinterpreted what they saw. I heard nothing that resembled the voice; no ill-intended tones, no whispered threats, nothing. There wasn't one iota of the voice I heard."

Peter backed me up about everything I said. Thankfully, about that time, the delivery guy showed up bringing our dinner, signaling a perfect time for a break. It surprised me to find the table already set, waiting for us. Uncle Charlie hardly ever participated in such formalities, so I looked over at Moira and gave her a thumbs up.

In a matter of minutes, we were filling our plates with the mouthwatering food from Uncle Charlie's favorite restaurant. After a while, once the hunger had subsided, the conversation picked back up again. This time we kept it more general as if by some unspoken agreement to leave the talk of murder behind while we ate.

When we finished, Uncle Charlie got up and started to clear the table, but before he could go any farther, Peter pulled out a piece of tin foil from his pocket. Clearing his throat, he motioned for me to hold up my hand, and there he placed the shiny foil package. I carefully peeled back the layers of tin foil to find a beautiful gold chain with a piece of lightning rock welded in between gold metal strands. The piece was beautiful, and I knew without asking that this was the piece Peter had pocketed when it had broken off the larger rock the lifeguards had given me the other day. The contrast of the gold against the small part he had saved accented the unique shape and showed where it had crystallized from the heat of the lightning, giving it an almost mystical look. As a necklace, it had become a thing of beauty.

"Peter, it's beautiful! How did you get this done so quickly?"

"Roger's sister does jewelry work, so I kinda passed it off to him and told him what I wanted. It seemed you had such a strong reaction to that rock, I thought it might comfort you to have a piece with you at all times."

As I took the necklace out of the tinfoil, I instantly realized he was right. I could feel the warmth as my finger touched the rock, and I could almost feel it humming with electricity.

Before I had the chance to thank him, Moira reached over and held it in her hand. She gave Peter a nod of approval and stood up to help me put it on. I at once experienced a strong mystic connection, as it met the skin of my throat. It felt like a part of me, almost vibrating with my heartbeat. The headache that had started earlier diminished as if by magic, and I felt the tension rush from me. It was almost as if the stone became a magnet, pulling all my pains and worries towards it, leaving me peaceful and clear-headed.

Uncle Charlie gave Peter a thump on the back as approval as we all walked to the living room. We'd just gotten comfortable when Charlie asked about the list of items he had wanted from the General Store.

"Over there, Uncle Charlie," I said as I motioned to the bag that Peter had left by the front door.

After rummaging through the bag, he sighed with annoyance, "Mac, did you forget to pick up the batteries I had asked for?"

"No, I had it on the counter, paid for it, and I thought Melissa put them in the bag."

"It's not here, Mac. I don't know where they are, but they're not in this bag."

I groaned with frustration. I knew that Uncle Charlie expected us to go back and get them.

"Oops, sorry about that. I'll run back. I'm not sure what happened, but don't worry about it. I'll take care of it. Let's take a walk, Peter, and work off dinner. You two relax, we'll be back in no time."

Uncle Charlie didn't try to dissuade me. Instead he sat on the couch next to Moira, looking content. I shrugged my shoulders and hauled myself to my feet. Glancing at Peter, I could see he was way too comfortable, and I grabbed his arm and pulled.

"Come on, mister, don't get too comfortable. You're just as much at fault as I am, we both should pay more attention."

With a grimace, he got to his feet, complaining he'd overeaten. I tickled him, as I told him that was even more reason to go with me and walk off his meal. With a laugh and a wave, we left the two sitting on the couch, already discussing a movie they had both seen.

It didn't take long to get to the General Store, as we walked at a good clip. With arms around each other, Peter reached out and tasseled my hair, something he knew I hated and I gave him a playful shove in return. Rather than letting me pull out of his arms, he tightened his embrace and leaned in to give me a light kiss on the forehead. If I had thought fast enough, I could have easily made it a kiss on the lips, but I lost the chance.

When we reached the store, I asked Melissa's assistant if we had left anything behind earlier.

"Oh, yes, you did. I put the bag aside for you under the counter. Hang on a second, I'll get it." As she turned around, the chimes on the door rang. Before I could see who walked into the store, a pain shot through my leg, and I instinctively grabbed the necklace for support. The voice this time seemed even angrier, and low pitched with frustration.

"Enough! This is going to end. If I can't have Peter, neither can you!"

I looked around, trying to find who it was. Melissa was at the ice cream counter, waiting on a customer. I saw Gloria had walked in, now heading over to the paint supplies as she looked at a list in her hands. It couldn't have been from her either. Then I looked over towards the sidewalk, and there Judy stood, looking in the window at us. But she didn't seem at all upset and she even smiled, waving at me when our eyes caught.

This was crazy. All three of the women were around me as I heard the voice, but I couldn't pinpoint which woman it came from. Which one wanted Peter?

Chapter 26

With a shake of my head, as if to knock some reasoning into it, I saw the clerk waiting for me. I thanked her and took the bag she held out for me. It amazed me that neither my hands nor my voice shook. As I turned to leave, I noticed that both Melissa and Gloria had acknowledged Peter and me with a wave. But with no words spoken, I couldn't compare voices. I needed to get out of there quickly, and I grabbed Peter's hand to head to the front door. My head pounded, and my heart raced. I'm not sure if the necklace intensified my reaction or if it was because all three women were in one spot. With the anger hidden so well, it created an evil atmosphere; only I could feel the effects of such hatred, and it threatened to overwhelm me.

When we walked out, we headed directly to the beach. This was our spot of solitude, and I needed the calmness of the waves crashing on the shore before I headed back to talk to Uncle Charlie and Moira about what had happened.

Peter sat by my side, holding my hand. "What happened in there, Mac? You almost went white on me, I thought you were going to pass out."

"It was the voice again, Peter. It was so strong, I thought it was going to take my breath away or make my heart explode—one or the other. She hides her feelings from the public, but the voice that's in her head is filled with passion and emotion. And I have proof it's in her head because not one of them said a word to us."

Peter turned to face me and held both of my hands, not allowing me to break eye contact. "Mac, is this too much for you? Your reaction scared me." He gulped and I swore his lip trembled a little. "I don't want you to get hurt. Let's walk away and let the police handle it."

"We can't do that, Peter, we're too invested into this already. We have the upper hand, so we've got to finish this through, and we need to do it fast. Something's going to happen, I just know it."

Peter knew better than to argue with me. We've known each other too long to play games. It made no sense to fight my resolve because I was determined to do it with or without his help. I hoped he realized that what I was doing was for him, and me. And for us.

"Okay, if this is something we have to do, then we have to do it. But we will go about it smartly. There will be no taking any chances, I want nothing to happen to you. I prefer to stay on this side of the grave too when it comes right down to it."

Smiling at his attempt at humor, I gave his hand a squeeze. "Let's get this to Uncle Charlie and let the two of them know what happened. We need to come up with a plan, and we need to get it into action. Now that we're pretty sure it's one of the three, we need to bring them out and find out exactly which one it is."

As we walked back to Uncle Charlie's, I wondered if he held my hand for appearance's sake or if he was getting used to the feel of my hand in his. I definitely enjoyed it. At least something good was coming out of this.

When we arrived at Uncle Charlie's, Moira knew immediately that something had happened. She rushed down the steps to meet us and placed both her hands on either side of my face.

"Whatever happened, you handled it well, Mackenzie. You're learning to hone in on your abilities." She lightly touched the necklace that hung around my neck. "Peter's gift is helping. Did you noticed, more of the sand has crystallized since you left."

Peter leaned in to look at the necklace. Moira was right, I could see more evidence of crystallization. It seemed to work from the inside of the rock, and the area that was already crystallized had turned a slight shade of blue. I'm not sure what it all meant, but the necklace was reading my reactions. Did it give me any added strength? I didn't care, I was just glad to have it.

Peter told them all that had happened, letting me try to relax for a moment. When he finished, Uncle Charlie took the bag from me and looked inside it. He mumbled the batteries weren't worth what he had put me through, and he shook his head. Moira reached over and squeezed his arm for reassurance. I could see the two of them were becoming good friends and seemed to have a special connection. I smiled to myself, wondering if Uncle Charlie even realized how close he was getting to Moira. He deserved a special relationship, and I hope that Moira would be the one to offer it. She was becoming an important part of my life too.

We talked long after the sun had set, still sitting on the porch, drinking iced tea. Together, we had hashed out a plan, and we were eager for the next day when we could put it into action.

Chapter 27

We met on the beach early the next morning. It was our regular routine, and we didn't want to be doing anything out of the ordinary. Moira joined us and, although Uncle Charlie wanted to, he couldn't get out of a court appearance he had that morning.

As we walked along the shoreline, Roger and some of his friends joined us A few moments later, two other off-duty lifeguards were there as well. Putting my hands on my hips, I looked at Peter, knowing he was behind this.

"Okay, Peter, what have you done?"

"Recruitment, Mackenzie. It's clear what Peter has done, and I think it's a lovely idea," Moira answered for Peter.

"I thought it might be smart for a few recruits to have our backs. We're not sure which one of us is a target, and we know we must split up to draw the murderer out. I got to thinking, why should we split up and sit there all alone, an easy target for anybody with murderous intent? So, I made a few calls, called in some favors and, with little arm twisting, got these guys to help us. Between everyone here, you and I should be under somebody's surveillance constantly while we put our plan into action. Everyone has cell phones and is willing to do what it takes to keep another murder from happening." Peter flashed a sincere smile at the guys around us, "Thanks, my friends, for giving up your day off."

I looked around me at the friends who cared enough to put their life on the line and felt tears well up in my eyes.

"This wasn't part of the plan, Peter, we weren't supposed to get anybody else involved, or put anybody else in danger. But I must admit, it feels good knowing others have my back and that somebody will be looking out for both of us."

"Yeah, I figured you'd come around. And let's face it, Mac, you're more of a potential target than me."

I had already figured that out, but now I was wondering how much Peter had told our friends. Did they know I heard voices? Was I going to be looked at as some weirdo?

As if he had read my mind, Peter gave me a quick hug and whispered in my ear to reassure me. "They've only been told what's necessary, Mac. I told them you've been threatened, but they don't know-how, and they don't know how you found out about the threats. Your secret's safe." He hugged me close to his chest and I had to blink back tears that he was so protective. I felt as if a great weight was off my shoulders and I whispered," thank you."'

Seeing everybody was anxious to get to work, we laid out our plan. It didn't take long, and within fifteen minutes, everybody was going to their designated spots to wait and watch what would happen next.

Moira was the last to leave us, and before she walked away, she touched the necklace around my neck and whispered, "believe in yourself." I didn't know if I could, but I would try my best. This would end today before somebody else got hurt or killed.

Peter put his arm around my shoulders and I realized that more would end than just an investigation. Once we discovered who the murderer was, and all this was laid to rest, there would be no reason for Peter to pretend to be my boyfriend. I felt a little heartbroken. I truly enjoyed all the attention I was getting from Peter. Whether it was real or fake, I treasured every moment of it, and I didn't want to see it end. Maybe that was selfish of me, but that's just the way it was.

Peter pointed out a dolphin swimming on the horizon, bringing my attention back to him and away from my daydreams. Somehow everything would be all right. Catching sight of the dolphin made it so. I always believed if I saw something good and perfect in nature, then something good would happen that day. So, why should today be any different? Whether it be catching a murderer or having something more special come out of this friendship between Peter and me, there was no telling what the outcome would be, but something good would happen, thanks to that dolphin sighting.

Our first stop would set our plan in motion. It wasn't an elaborate plan, or mind-boggling, or even terribly ingenious, but we hoped it would work. The goal was to visit each of the three suspects and let it slip that Peter and I would be on our own for the day in separate places with easy access. If the killer was going to make her move, this would be the time.

As we walked into the coffee shop, I was surprised to see Peter's reinforcements already there. Roger and two of the other guys had ordered coffee and were sitting in strategic places within the coffee shop. From where they were seated, they could easily observe the comings and goings. I looked up at Peter in surprise, but he just grinned down at me and winked. Instantly, I knew this was part of his plan. As we moved from one location to another, there would be somebody behind to monitor the reaction and movements of the potential murderer.

Judy was working behind the counter rather than waiting tables, so we made sure that we ordered takeout, knowing that she would be stuck listening to us as she fulfilled our order. Peter started the game in motion as he turned to me and moaned out loud.

"I'm sure going to miss you this afternoon. Are you sure you need to go out to The Groves? You could wait, and I'll go with you. I need to drop off these documents, then my day is free."

"It would be nice, but there isn't enough time. By the time you drive south to drop those papers off at the construction site, I could be halfway out to The Groves. We would never have time to get both things done. We need to go our separate ways. We'll meet up later tonight. It'll be okay."

I smiled up at him, my voice sounding fake to me, and I was gagging at how sickening sweet I was being, but it had to be done. This had to be a convincing act.

From the corner of my eye, I noticed Judy was taking all of this in as we talked. She showed no outward reaction, but she wasn't missing anything either. She had caught every word we said, and I made sure she also caught the spontaneous kiss I gave Peter. I don't know who was more surprised when he turned his cheek at the last second, and my kiss landed on his lips. As I pulled away, he raised his eyebrows. For a moment, I forgot why we were there until Judy placed our to-go cups down in front of us, breaking the spell.

Peter was the first to react to the interruption. Reaching into a pocket, he pulled out his wallet and paid for our drinks, thanking Judy and wishing her a lovely day. There was nothing left for us to do except to go and hope the seed we had planted took root.

⟺⬤⟺

WE HAD HEARD FROM ONE lifeguard that Gloria had abandoned her usual spot on the Boardwalk and was painting at the park in the center of town, so that's where we headed next.

Once we reached the park, we wandered the pathways until we sighted Gloria in the distance, and then the show was on again. Holding hands, we made our way leisurely towards her. Once we reached her side, we watched Gloria paint for a few moments before I broke the silence.

"This is beautiful, Gloria. I've never seen you paint anything other than seascapes. Have you ever done any painting out at The Groves?" Nervousness had my two questions coming fast and without thought. I didn't allow her to answer me. Instead I kept talking. "I'm heading out to The Groves today. There are so many lovely spots that would make pretty paintings. And if you're lucky, you can catch some of the wildlife. The last time I was out there, I caught sight of a panther; she was beautiful. Of course, I didn't have my camera."

Gloria sighed and looked wistful. "Lucky you, I've yet to see a Florida panther in the wild." She hesitated long enough to add a new color to her paintbrush. "That's why I paint, my pictures are caught in my memories, so I don't need a camera. But I would love to see that panther. You must show me where in The Groves to go for the best things to paint."

"I'm sure Mac could show you the best places, most people don't even know are there. I wish I could go out there with her today, it's always so nice to spend time out there. But I'm stuck going to the construction site where the new hotel is being built for my father's client. Driving down south in the traffic is the last thing I want to do. It's a long drive by myself," Peter said.

She looked at both of us and it was clear she was wondering why Peter was bothering to give her so many details, but she made no comment. Instead, she concentrated on her painting. But I felt that she understood where we were going and that I would be alone. We had accomplished what we came to do and now there was only a third place to go before we set ourselves up as bait.

———◉———

WHEN WE REACHED THE General Store, we again saw some of our friends there inconspicuously shopping. With Melissa, there was no need to be subtle. She asked outright what our plans were for the day. Peter happily filled her in, playing the love-sick fool as he complained about being away from me for the day. Before Melissa could make any comment, the bells on the front door rang, and we turned as Detective Byrd entered the store.

I watched as he surveyed the area, taking it all in. He didn't miss anything, including Peter holding my hand. His eyebrows raised slightly, and he gave a slight nod as he caught me watching him.

"Well, the two of you will need a few supplies for your trips," said Melissa after she gave a wave to the detective, thinking he was just another customer coming in to buy some ice cream. "Peter, you need to make sure you've got something to eat and drink since you'll be on the road for so long. And Mac, I just ordered a new natural insect control that you should try when you go out to The Groves. You can be my guinea pig, so that I can let my customers know if it works. You know as well as I do, the mosquitoes are the worst out there, and if this stuff works, I'll be able to sell it like hotcakes." Melissa, eager to make a sale, didn't realize that she was giving Detective Byrd the information on our plans for the day.

Chapter 28

"The detective seemed surprised we were a couple," I said after we were outside. "You'd think he would have heard about it through the gossip going on in town. He didn't miss much either, he was thoroughly checking out everybody in the store, almost as if he had his own agenda. Somehow, I think he would still like to place the blame of Isabella's murder on you. He was sure listening in on what Melissa said, too."

"That's fine, it means one more person knows where we're going. And this person carries a gun, even better. So, it's a good thing he's aware of our plans." Pausing a moment, Peter looked at me and got serious.

"Mac, promise me you won't take any chances today. You are the prime target, and I don't want anything to happen to you."

I gave him a reassuring hug, promising I would be careful, and I made him make the same promise. He did, and after tucking a loose strand of my hair behind my ear, he bent down and gave me a tender kiss.

"There, our promises have been sealed with a kiss. I think that's more appropriate than the pinky-swear we used to do when we were younger."

I grinned at the memory of our old promises and understood with his kiss, no matter what happened, our friendship would always be rock solid. I just hoped that it'd mean as much later.

"At least I have an advantage," I teased, "if she talks, I'll hear her."

"Not to doubt your abilities, but so far that hasn't been working out as well as we hoped. Be careful." He returned my hug, and after I told Peter I wanted to walk home, he walked towards his car.

I waved when he caught me following his progress towards his car, and he returned the wave with a salute for encouragement. After he pulled out into the street and headed south, I made my way home to pick up my car to head west.

Chapter 29

For me, the drive out to The Groves was something I'd always enjoyed. The route follows the coast as it turns into the Florida wilderness. I loved coming out here, and I always had, ever since I was a little girl. Just as my parents had when they were children.

Back then, not only were there orange groves to visit, and freshly picked sweet juicy fruit to enjoy, but also alligator wrestling hosted by the local Native American tribe in their full costumes. If you were lucky, you could observe the beekeepers harvest the honey from the hives. Once you've sampled this distinctive honey, you were more than willing to endure a few bee stings. My mouth salivated. I could still taste the local orange blossom honey.

Along with the food goodies and entertainment, there was always touristy items to buy. The breeze would make the hand-crafted wind chimes of seashells call your attention, and the unique sound and shapes would invite you to their display. Sometimes they would hang from the eves of the packing house, other times from the trees. Table-toppers made of beautiful mirrors edged in coral, alligator heads, and the ever-popular tables made from Cypress knees could always be found to help the tourist spend their money.

To a young girl it was fun and adventurous, and I had looked forward to every time I went out to the Groves. When my parents were alive, it was a great family adventure. After they passed, Uncle Charlie would take me. With him, I always seemed to learn something new about the history of Florida, turning my adventures into lessons about life in old Florida.

As I grew older, I appreciated more of the natural beauty of The Groves. I learned to look for signs of Florida life that didn't necessarily pertain to tourist traps. Even in the heat of a Florida summer, there were treasures abound. A sharp eye and keen hearing often brings things into focus a casual observer might not notice.

The section of The Groves I was heading for had a beautiful nature trail left to grow wild. It no longer produced citrus fruit for harvest, since most of the citrus had died off when native plants had reclaimed the land. The owners had added palms and tropical flowers. The birds and wind did their part, carrying seeds from ferns and wild orchids, creating a local attraction that many tourists weren't aware even existed. Wild vines, brush, and palmetto palms took over large areas, but when the county took the land back, they made attempts at keeping the undergrowth contained. Much of the land had even returned to its boggy state, and the county now provided man-made boardwalks and bridges to get from one area to the next without having to wade through the waters filled with critters that called the area home.

Even though the mosquitoes and other bugs were a problem, if you spent any length of time, I stilled enjoyed coming. I always felt a bit of solace as I walked through the old Citrus Groves, often wondering if it had appeared the same for those early Florida settlers.

Too bad I wasn't here for enjoyment today, but instead I had to keep my guard up and pay attention. I was setting a trap for a killer, and I couldn't allow myself to get lulled into the peacefulness that awaited me.

When I reach the parking lot, I pulled into a secluded spot and turned off the engine. The parking lot was deserted, except for two cars. I jumped a little when my cell phone vibrated. It was from Peter.

"Hey."

"Hey. Are you there yet?"

"Just got here. You?"

"You'll never guess what happened to me."

"What?"

Peter explained that before he had arrived at the construction site, he noticed a car was following him. He didn't think it was any big deal, as a lot of people went in and out of a hardware store next to his dad's client's construction site.

"But Mac, listen to this. When I pulled into the site and parked, I nearly fell over when I got out."

"Don't leave me in suspense, Peter!" I admonished. "Why, who was following you?"

"It was Gloria."

"What? No! What did she want?"

Peter told me what happened next.

"Gloria assured me she wasn't stalking me but needed to talk." Peter cleared his throat and paraphrased what Gloria had said.

"She felt something was off today. Gloria said there seemed to be a charge in the atmosphere that felt dangerous. She couldn't explain what is causing it, but felt it in the store and was sure it was direct towards you and me. Gloria swore there was a black aura building, ready to burst." Peter gave a nervous laugh and I knew he felt uncomfortable with Gloria's talk of auras and then continued. "She insisted that we should be separated. She followed me to persuade me to drive out to the Groves and find you. Having the detective in the store made her feel edgy as well and she was certain something was going to happen."

I was silent as I digested his words.

"Mac? You there?"

"Yes, sorry. And then what happened?"

"I tried to get more information, but Gloria said she was basing everything on a feeling she experienced."

I must have sighed out loud with frustration because the next few sentences he said with emotion.

"Look, I don't understand everything that is happening right now, but we need to accept Gloria's advice. What more do we have?"

"You're right."

"Don't worry, Mac. Remember the pinky-swear that we'd protect each other through thick and thin-"

"Oh, I thought you-" I began, wanting to remind him that he kissed me earlier in lieu of a pinkie swear.

"Don't worry," he said, obviously mistaking my hesitation for worry instead of wanting to feel his kiss again, "I'm heading out to you now."

I wasn't going to hold my breath waiting for him, though. He was over an hour away.

The late afternoon sun beat through the back window, and I rolled down all the windows and felt the humidity hit me like a wet towel being thrown against my face. In a matter of seconds, the coolness from the air conditioning of the car disappeared, but I heard what was going on around me, so I put up with this minor discomfort.

A cry of an eagle reached me. Peering up, I followed her flight through the trees until she arrived at a nest high in the scrub pines. It didn't take long for a second sound to make itself known, and with an irritated wave of my hand, I tried to brush away the mosquitoes that seemed to come out of nowhere. I knew from experience the mosquitoes here were fierce, and I reached over and grabbed the insect repellent.

I climbed out of the car and sprayed every inch of exposed skin, making sure to keep those pesky little bugs away. I stretched from the long ride and looked around me a little closer. The plant life was lush from the recent rains, and there was a clean scent to the area, not the dusty summer air that caused fits of sneezes.

I studied the sky to see where the sun was and judged there was only an hour left of daylight. Out there amongst all the trees, it would get dark quickly and the overhead canape of foliage was so thick that the moonlight wouldn't provide any light. As much as I didn't want a confrontation with anybody, I hoped whoever took our bait would arrive soon. There would be no advantage to a showdown in the dark.

I should stay close to the car, but I also didn't want to sit there like a sitting duck, prime for target practice. I locked up the car and headed towards a small narrow pathway through the foliage. I remembered exactly where it led and meandered down it while I waited. It was the perfect solution; at the end of the path there was a large clearing, but along the pathway were many places I could hide if I needed to. The clearing would be perfect if I needed to confront the killer, but hopefully, it wouldn't come to that, of course. As I started down the path, I wondered where Peter's reinforcements were. I didn't dwell on that thought; I had confidence they would show. When I heard a car door slam, followed by a second, I sighed, relieved, and assumed the recruitments had arrived. With a more confident step, knowing I had somebody watching out for me, I continue down the path.

Chapter 30.

The hammock could be a peaceful place and lull you into an almost trance-like calmness. The local wildlife chattered among themselves and ignored my intrusion; they sensed I was no threat. As I continued down the path, I identified the different songs of a mockingbird as he followed me, and the rustling of the many lizards that scurried in the undergrowth. I was aware of larger animals wandering in the area, but they kept their distance. I watched the flight of two butterflies and they settled momentarily on a bright hibiscus flower before moving on to the next patch of flowers, small delicate ground orchids.

I caught the scent of old citrus that had gone wild from years of not being harvested. The humidity had a way of holding the scents close to the ground, and I could even smell the boggy earth, rich with nutrients and moisture.

There under the canape of tree branches, the air seemed a tad cooler, and dusk seemed to settle quicker than I thought it would. Out in the open, it would be brighter, but the shadows ran deep there, and I picked up my pace to reach the opening.

When I reached the clearing, I was enchanted to see a family of raccoons playing on a couple of old logs from a fallen tree. They stopped their play when I walked out from the pathway, but after a moment, they went back to their playtime. I was unimportant in the scheme of their daily routine, and they were having too much fun to give me a second thought. Keeping my distance, I walked the perimeter of the opening, taking in the locations of a few trails that headed out in opposite directions.

I was sure some of the guys must be behind me, and that made me confident in my safety as I walked around the area. Maybe I became overconfident, and I should have checked to be sure it was the guys, but I knew how long it took to drive out there, and no one had passed me in route. Still, it surprised me none of them called out, letting me know of their arrival.

Now that I was out in the open, I could feel a slight breeze, and I heard the leaves rustling as the wind moved through the branches. The clouds gathered in the sky, making the early evening sky even darker. Distant flashes of lightning raced from cloud to cloud as if they contained messages sent by the Gods. I hoped I wouldn't have to stay out here once it turned completely dark. Not only would I need to worry about a murderer, but there were other nightcrawlers and nocturnal animals that called the hammock home. I didn't want to come face to face with any of them. No, the hammock and grove took on a whole new feeling after sunset.

I heard the footsteps of somebody coming up the trail. I started to call out to them but stopped before the words left my mouth. Instead of my protectors, I saw the outline of a woman walking towards me. This couldn't be good. As if to confirm I was in a tight spot, a bolt of lightning exploded across the sky, illuminating the clearing for a moment, letting me see the face of the killer.

The heat around my ankle increased, and it slowly turned to pain. Now it was apparent I faced danger-I was learning to recognize the signals my body sent me much faster. Not that it would do me any good now. I slowed my breathing and willed my heartbeat to settle back to its normal pace. I needed to be in full control of my body, hoping that the signals I received would protect me. Concentrating, I listened for the sign that the others had arrived. Nothing, only a woman's voice.

When I heard the woman's voice this time, it wasn't in my head, but ringing out in the clear summer air. It didn't matter if it was in my head or spoken out loud; I recognized it immediately. She spoke from where she stood, watching me from the shadows of the pathway.

"Why did you have to take him from me, Mackenzie? Why couldn't you just be satisfied with having Peter as a friend? I like you, I really do, but I can't have you interfering with my relationship with Peter. He's mine. He always will be mine. And once you're gone, I will make him realize that."

Yes, it was the voice I kept hearing. It matched perfectly. Filled with tones of anger and hatred, and it chilled me to have these feelings directed at me. But standing in front of me was another surprise. This was not the woman I expected, looking at me with an expression that had me shaking down to my toes. No, she was the one I would have expected the least.

Chapter 31

J udy Nick was planning on killing me. And, she looked determined. Her words sounded cold and emotionless, frightening me more than if she had screamed. There was a calmness about her, as if her mind had already played out the actions she planned to take. She came to a stop and watched me as if waiting to see what I would do next.

Instead of turning and running blindly, I took in the details of Judy's appearance, trying to see if she had a weapon. Glancing around, I analyzed what I could use as a weapon to protect myself. A few solid branches were lying on the ground waiting to be picked up and wielded as a weapon. I already knew that she could bludgeon someone to death because that's what she did to Isabella. I needed to make sure I didn't come to the same fate.

As I kept my eye on her, I took a tentative step closer to one of the pathways, hoping that she wouldn't notice my movement. Judy gave no sign she saw my first step, so I took another, making the steps small, swaying back and forth as though I was nervous, praying the movement would hide my advancement. After a few such moments, I was close enough to the pathway, and I figured if I moved fast, I would be able to lose myself in the wilderness. But before I attempted my escape, I wanted to find out why she killed Isabella.

"You followed Peter and Isabella that night, didn't you, Judy?" I kept my voice steady, not wanting to startle or anger her.

"They never even saw me," she said, her voice confident. "It's amazing how a quiet person can become invisible. Most people aren't even aware of my presence outside the coffee shop. I'm one of the nobody people. Those silent people that wait on you, and then, when you walk away, we disappear, and you don't give us a second thought.

But Isabella was sure thinking about me that night. I don't believe Peter was that serious about her. Look at how quickly he hooked up with you. I always knew the two of you had a special friendship. I just wish you had kept it a friendship, and not taken Isabella's place, Mackenzie. You've always been nice to me and I really hate to do this to you." I followed her arm's movement in fixated horror as it came out from behind her back holding a large butcher knife.

So, she would not beat me with a stick, she planned to stab me to death. Well I had news for her; I wasn't going down without a fight.

I prayed the recruits were on their way if they weren't already there. I realized if I wanted to stay alive until they got to me, I needed to keep her talking. I needed to keep her from taking any action. I took another step to my right, but this time she saw my movement.

"Let's not try anything funny, Mackenzie, I don't want to have to run and chase you. One way or another you will die today. You may as well do it with some dignity."

I stopped in my tracks. Judy was serious, and she would kill me, I saw it in her eyes. Gone was the timid woman with the hesitant smile. Standing in front of me, knife in hand, was a stone-cold killer.

She was right, I needed to do this with dignity, but it wasn't the type of dignity she was thinking of; I was going to do it with the dignity of a fighter. I would stand up for myself and fight to stay alive. There would be no going down with a mere whimper. If she was going to kill me, she would have to fight me to my last breath.

I looked around me; the cloud cover was making it seem even darker. If I could stall long enough for either help to arrive, or it to get dark enough to somehow give me an advantage, I might survive this. The trick was to keep her talking, to keep her thinking about Peter and not about me.

"If you love Peter so much, then why are you doing this? Do you think he will applaud your efforts to get him to yourself? You're not going to turn him away from me this way, Judy. No, instead, he will notice you for all the wrong reasons. And they won't be the loving reasons you think."

She gave a little shrug of her shoulders. It was apparent her own passion for Peter was blocking any common sense. But I needed to keep trying.

"Think for a minute, Judy. You said yourself that Peter and I have a unique friendship. How is he going to feel about you if you killed me? Every time he looks at you, he will remember that you are the person who ended my life. Do you imagine for a second those are going to be loving thoughts? And what about your own life? You've already murdered somebody; how does that weigh on your shoulders? You might be full of passion right now for Peter, but what happens when that guilt eats at you? Will you blame Peter?"

I had her interest, and she hesitated. Whether she would feel any guilt was beyond me. I saw she was barely beginning to understand what she had done.

Judy's arm holding the knife wavered for a moment and she tilted her head as if pondering what I had said. I was hoping I was getting through to her. Deciding to risk her anger, I pushed it a little farther.

"What kind of relationship can you build with the man you love, with that dark evil hanging over you? Sooner or later one of you will resent the other. Are you prepared for that?"

Judy weighed my words, but then slowly smiled and shook her head. "Peter will learn to love me the way I love him. There won't be any resentment. We'll work through everything—our love will carry us through."

"You're not being realistic. I'm sorry, Judy, but it's simply a fantasy you've created in your mind. I know Peter better than anyone, and I tell you this: he'll never be able to forgive you. Even if it's not me, the idea you killed somebody in his name will turn him against you."

The girl in front of me only heard part of what I said. I think because in her mind, she had already created a picture-perfect world for her and Peter to live in, and nothing I said would shake that reality for her. She was shaking her head at me in pity and her smile became taut and almost evil.

"Poor Mackenzie, you don't understand-true love will win over everything. Yes, you and Peter have a special relationship, you've been friends forever, but what Peter and I have is much deeper. It's overwhelmingly encompassing, and it will surpass any negative feelings. And once you're out of the way, Peter will forget all about you, and it'll just be the two of us. No more Mackenzie. Only me for Peter to love."

Words failed me. I had no idea what to say to her. How do you argue with somebody so delusional? Yet I must argue, I needed to use words to save myself-they were my only weapon.

Chapter 32

"Judy, where do you think your relationship with Peter is going?" I let that question sink in before I asked my next one. "What do you think the future holds for the two of you?"

Once she started to answer, I kept probing her. In her mind, she had the entire future planned for the two of them, and she was more than happy to share her dreams with me. As she talked, her voice took on a dreamy tone, almost as if she were reciting a beloved fairytale. The more details she wove, the more I saw she had created a complete story for her and Peter. I was determined that her fairytale wouldn't end with the evil witch winning.

As she talked, the surrounding woods became quiet. Dusk settled, and the animals were burring into their nests for the evening. Where was everyone? I had never felt so alone in my life. The rescue I wanted didn't seem like it would show up any time soon. I needed to act now if I was going to make it out of this mess. I took a couple of the deep breaths that Moira had trained me to do, centering myself. By the third breath, Judy's voice seemed to come from a distance. My skin tingled and I felt the breeze on my skin with such clarity I swear I could name each hair on my arm as it stood up. Tension filled the atmosphere that resembled an approaching storm. It took a few moments to realized that I had become the source of the tension. With each breath, tension poured from my body, building up like an electric current.

Judy was so wrapped up in her fairytale world, she wasn't aware of the change. She kept talking, losing focus on me. But as she became unfocused, I became more in-tune with what was going on around me. I sensed just when the lighting would strike and I felt it from my ankle to my head. And when the first lightning bolt raced across the sky, I couldn't be sure if it came from the clouds or my soul.

The bolt was bright, almost a neon blue, bright enough to affect Judy's vision and take her attention away from me. When I saw her glance at the sky, it was my moment to act. It might be the only one I would get, and I didn't hesitate. With speed I didn't even know I possessed, I turned and ran down the path to my right. It wasn't much of a path, and I found that out the hard way as I tripped over broken branches and debris.

I didn't get too far before Judy's cry of rage reached me before I heard the sounds of her fumbling footsteps following me. She was having a tough time finding and following the path. I slowed my movements to a more sleuth-like pace, trying to keep my exact location hidden from her for as long as possible. I took my steps with care, and it seemed as if the pathway opened for me

Oddly enough, the birds and small animals kept silent as well, almost as if they wanted to keep my passage secret. The cat and mouse game continued. Judy had slowed her wild pace to listen for my movements. She might be delusional in her love for Peter, but she was a smart woman. The phrase 'crazy like a fox' gave me a mental slap; it became clear she knew how to track her prey.

I sat on my heels to get my bearings, and I caught the sound I had longed for earlier.

Peter's voice rang out. "Mac, where are you?"

Other voices rang out, searching for me. I realized Judy would fight us all to win her reward.

Then I sensed Moira, more than I heard her, but I heard another woman's voice too, one that I couldn't identify. As I listened, I picked out a few male voices as they joined in the search. Better late than never, I thought. I almost groaned out loud when I realized the voices were splitting up and spreading into different directions. What a mistake! It would be easy for Judy to attack them, one by one. She was sly, and I pictured her picking off her prey, until only Peter remained.

I had to do something. Only I knew how dangerous Judy was, and the crazy state of her mind. Without thinking twice, I worked my way in the direction of my friends' voices. If I could get between her and the rest, maybe I could do something. What I didn't know.

Closing my eyes and concentrating, I sensed Peter's presence. I wanted to go to him first, but I instinctively knew he was in the least danger. Judy would not harm him-unless he rejected her. I needed to get to the others first, and together we could stop the woman. I took another deep breath, eyes still closed, and felt Moira almost reaching out to me. She could help me end this, I was sure of it.

I concentrated on Moira's vibe, and soon I worked my way towards where she would be. The connection between us never felt stronger than it did right now. It seemed as if Moira guided me through the wilderness to her side.

As I stood by Moira, I held my fingers to my lips. She nodded and then pointed off to the right and mouthed 'Peter.' I needed to figure out a way to intercept the killer and stop her before she used the knife she had threatened me with. What I would do after that, I didn't have a clue, but I couldn't wait around for a brilliant plan to show itself. This would have to be ad-lib, a by-the-seat-of-your-pants solution.

"Mac!"

I was going over my options, slim as they were, trying to decide what would be the safest way to get the situation under control, with no one getting hurt. I had a rough plan ready when Peter called out my name. When I heard his voice, it became clear nothing I had thought of would be sufficiently heroic.

As I turned toward his voice, I gasped as I was hit with a sharp stabbing pain around my scar. I stumbled in pain, overwhelmed by the intensity of it. It felt like I was being struck by another bolt of lightning.

"Mackenzie, breathe." Moira's gentle voice broke through my pain, and the soothing touch of her hand on my arm steadied me.

Her touch felt warm on my skin and almost seemed to radiate strength. I took a deep, calming, centered breath, and the pain subsided. As my head cleared, Judy's voice reached me, passion ringing through, as if she stood right next to me.

"You're mine now, Peter. I won't let anything come between us. Nothing. No one. This time I will end it so we can begin our new life together."

I was moving before I even thought. Peter couldn't possibly understand how delusional she was, or how convinced she was it would all end with the happily ever after ending she imagined. My feet carried me with speed down the small path, as if being pulled towards Judy and the ultimate showdown we would face.

My confrontation with Judy happened sooner than I expected. As I rounded a small curve in the pathway, I came face to face with the woman. I wasn't sure which of us was more surprised, and for a nano-second, we stood as if frozen, staring at each other. We stood so close that even in the dusky darkness of the evening light, I clearly made out her features. I watched as her mouth dropped open in surprise and then in an instant, her mouth grimaced, and her face became red with rage and determination. I shivered in fear. This was not the friendly little coffee barista that served my favorite hazelnut coffee blend every morning. There was a madness in her eyes that would probably scare a trained psychiatrist. And she directed it at me. She would kill me if I didn't stop her. There was no waiting to be rescued; the next few seconds would decide who would walk away from here alive.

I thought of all that had happened in the last few days, and I surprised myself when I concluded that I could handle whatever happened next. I became more aware of myself and my surroundings than I ever remembered doing in the past. A random thought broke through, reminding me to breathe deeply and concentrate. I wasn't sure what to focus on, or what the results might be, but it was worth a try.

As I inhaled, I pictured Shaylee, swatting at a dragonfly in my garden. The picture changed, and the dragonfly seemed to have a glow about it, and Shaylee's movement seemed to be less of a swat and more of a command. I felt the same peace take hold of me that I often found in my garden, and when I exhaled, the fear left with my breath. I inhaled a second time, not breaking eye contact with Judy. The atmosphere crackled, and I heard distant thunder. But I didn't look away. As I exhaled, the ground seemed to have a slight glow under the wandering foliage of the hammock floor. It must have been the way the last drop of light from the setting sun hit the foliage, and it faded.

Judy gave a growl of rage and lunged at me. Her action was so fast, I barely had a moment to sidestep her, losing my balance in the process. She didn't hesitate and had followed my downward movement to crouch over me, keeping herself high enough over me to get the leverage needed for a firm, tightening grip around my neck. As her fingers tightened, I heard Peter calling out. Judy heard him too, and with an evil grin she bent forward and whispered in my ear.

"He's mine now, Mac."

Her voice matched the voice I had heard in my head, and I acted without thinking of the danger, wanting to protect the man I loved. With all the strength I could muster, I used my hands to break the grip around my throat, thrashing wildly as her hands slipped. My movements worked, and she lost her hold on me. In one swift movement, I pushed my upper torso up and gave the woman who now sat on my stomach a head-butt so hard that I saw stars.

Judy was dazed and held her head, moaning. I twisted my body to get her off me before she came to her senses.

"What the-?" Judy said in confusion. I peered in the same direction she was looking. It wasn't stars that I saw, but fireflies.

They rose from the ground and moved in a magical dance, coming closer to us. Some seemed to wrap me in protection, while others darted madly at Judy, causing her to wave frantically at them as if they were stinging bees. The glow from the fireflies seemed to intensify, and they moved in closer to her. A few hovered around me, as if for protection, gently floating around me. One seemed to hover in front of me for a moment as if trying to catch my attention. I looked closer at it, noticing that its form seemed different from how I remembered a firefly looking.

"Mac! Thank God you're okay." Peter reached my side and wrapped me in his strong arms, kissing the top of my head in relief.

Moira appeared and gasped at the sight of the hundreds of fireflies swarming around Judy. Moira stayed silent for a moment, and then she looked over at me and smiled. With a wave of her arm, the glow dissipated, as if on command.

Roger and Gloria burst through the undergrowth and, moving without hesitation, they rushed forward to apprehend Judy.

"Be careful, she has a knife," I warned them.

With that knowledge, Roger took the lead and hauled Judy to her feet. With speed and skill, Gloria removed her scarf she had tied around her waist and used it to bind Judy's hands behind her back.

"We'll take her back out to the parking lot where she can't get into any trouble," Roger told us, giving Judy a push in that direction. Peter ignored the pleading look Judy cast his way. Instead, he put his hands on either side of my face and looked deeply into my eyes.

"Tell me you're okay. I couldn't take it if she hurt you, Mac."

Without waiting for an answer, he kissed me. It was not the kiss a man would give his buddy or friend. This kiss was full of passion, starting forceful and ending tenderly, taking both of us by surprise. Peter broke away, but not before he placed another tender kiss on my lips, with the promise of much more to come. But before we could explore our feelings deeper, Moira interrupted.

"We'd better follow them. There is evil out here in the night hours. The evil we do not want to confront. Lead the way, Peter."

Moira's words were practical, but I was so desperate to find out more about where that kiss might be leading. Without allowing me to protest, Moira took each of us by the arm and headed towards the parking area.

Chapter 33

Moira led the way out, while Peter held my hand tightly. When we emerged from the deep shadows, it was to find a very different scene from the parking lot I had pulled into earlier. The parking lot seemed full, and as I watched, more cars pulled in, with tires screeching.

Roger and Gloria had subdued Judy, and when she saw Peter, her face lit up with joy and a passion I had never seen from her.

"Peter, you came for me." She cried out to him, taking a step towards us.

Roger pushed her back against the car, holding her arm so she couldn't escape. She glanced at Peter holding my hand and looked up, her eyes meeting mine. I saw tears roll down her cheeks, but she said nothing. There was no need, her thoughts came to me as clearly as if she spoke in my ear.

"I've lost him to you, Mackenzie."

There was pain and resolution in the voice, and part of my heart went out to her. I knew what it was like to love fiercely, not knowing if the other person returned those same feelings. Not that I would ever kill, but I could understand her heart break. She lowered her head in defeat.

"Mackenzie." the sound of my godfather's concerned voice distracted me from Judy, and I was amazed that he had his car door opened before he put it into park. He moved with a speed I hadn't seen him show in years. Moira stepped forward to calm him as another car pulled in with blue lights flashing.

Detective Byrd got out of his car at a slower pace, and he stopped short when he saw Roger restraining Judy. After taking in the situation in a swift glance, he motioned for one of the other officers on site to take the woman into custody.

"Counselor, I got your message about the murder being solved. Now I want to know what is happening. And why was I following behind you at eighty miles an hour?"

Uncle Charlie didn't give an apology for his speed, or for giving the detective such vague clues. He was too busy squeezing me until I could hardly breathe.

"Charlie, she's fine. You can let her go now. Mackenzie, tell us what happened." Moira's gentle voice calmed Uncle Charlie, and he gave a weak, embarrassed laugh, releasing me and taking a step back. I looked at the faces around me and saw they all wanted to find out what had happened between Judy and myself. But there were too many outsiders here for me to tell the whole tale. I did not want to be put in a second squad car and transported to the local hospital for a mental evaluation.

"Do you mind if I sit? It's been a little wild, and I could use a drink of water." I was stalling for time, and it worked. Detective Byrd sent one of his officers for a bottle of water while Peter and Uncle Charlie guided me to one of the picnic tables.

As we had sat down, there was a loud cry of surprise, and then the sound of a gunshot. As one, we jumped to our feet, ready to run. The sight in front of us stopped us in our tracks. Judy was holding a gun in her hand, pointing it at the unlucky police officer she had taken it from in a swift, unexpected movement. Moving a few steps away from him, she ordered all of us to not move. Waving the gun, she directed Roger and Gloria, along with the other police officers on the site to move in our direction. She was rounding us up like cattle; I only hoped that we weren't being rounded up for a slaughter.

When the others reached our table, she shouted an order for all of us to sit. Then she spoke again, and we could faintly hear her, but the message was clear. We weren't to move or she would shoot us.

"I loved him with all I had. There is nothing left."

Her thoughts came to me before she took the action that caught the others by surprise. In one motion, she raised her arm, pointed the gun at Peter, and pulled the trigger.

Her aim was high, and the shot flew wildly into the air above us. Everyone ducked for protection, but I didn't move. She couldn't kill Peter, she loved him too much. Instead, she took advantage of the distraction and turned to run toward the thick glades. She threw the gun away before she slipped out of sight, leaving behind the only protection she would have from the wilds of the Florida night.

She was fast and had the advantage of distance on her side. In seconds, the darkness swallowed her up from our view. In his frustration, Detective Byrd barked out orders, and quickly organized a search team.

Peter and I stepped away from the others, needing to come to grips with what had just happened. We had each been spared tonight and were still a little dazed by the craziness. Peter pulled me in for a tight hug, holding me as if he needed to reassure himself we were still alive and well. After a few seconds, I tried to pull back, but although he loosened his hold, he didn't release me. When he finally spoke, his voice was raw with emotion.

"Mac, what happened tonight? Not only with Judy, but with you?" he asked, hesitating a moment as if unsure of what words to use before he continued. "What I saw out there was unreal. All those fireflies. They seemed to protect you, Mac. It's more than hearing voices, it's as if you had someone looking out for you. Someone other than Moira-I know that she's part of all of this."

"Not now, Peter. I'm not sure what happened out there either. But somehow, with Moira's help, it will all be revealed in the proper time." But Peter was right, I had felt a cloak of protection around me as if it came from nature itself. I couldn't explain it without asking Moira a few questions. Somehow, I was sure that her answers would only lead to more questions. I wasn't ready for that yet.

We heard a terrified woman's scream piercing the night, followed by an eerie silence. The silence was worse than the scream had been.

"I think this has just turned from a search and rescue to a search and recovery mission." Detective Byrd's somber announcement broke the silence. A chill raced up my back.

"I think it would be best if you all go home. I can get your statements tomorrow. Mackenzie, I want a full explanation of how you found out Judy Nick was the murderer. You're not telling me the whole story, so be prepared to do so tomorrow."

I nodded my understanding. It was not a nod of agreement. We would have to deal with that tomorrow. With a final look back towards the glades, Peter led me to Uncle Charlie's car. Without a word, Peter threw his keys to Gloria so she could drive his car, and then got in in the backseat with me. I cuddled into Peter's arms, feeling safe and warm. I reached for my necklace and held it tight. But I held onto Peter tighter.

The headlights cut a path through the darkness as we made our way home. The silence in the car matched the silence in my head. Judy's voice would no longer haunt me.

Epilogue

We sat under the gazebo in my garden and felt blessed to all be together. We had been through so much, but it only strengthened old relationships and created new friendships that would last forever.

I looked around at my friends and family, grateful that we had come through all of this safely. As if reading my mind, Peter put his arms around my shoulders. But I pulled away.

"We don't have to pretend anymore, Peter," I whispered, sadness lacing my voice.

" I'm not pretending, Mac," he whispered back.

As I smiled to myself, I wasn't sure what the future held, but I knew it wasn't the last of the voices I would hear, and I needed to prepare myself. With help from Moira, I would be better prepared the next time it happened. I settled in to get comfortable and relax with those around me. Shaylee jumped up on my lap, ready to get comfortable herself. She ears flickered when something caught her interest and she raised her paw to flick at something. I turned to see what she was looking at, but I wasn't quick enough. I looked down at the cat to find her looking up with me with her intelligent eyes that seemed to taunt me for missing what she had seen.

I reached over to scratch her behind the ears. Before long, I relaxed to the point of almost nodding off, letting the conversation flow around me.

Without warning, lightning raced across the sky in a brilliant show, arching from one cloud to another before finally coming down to earth. I was aware of the moment the lightning touched the ground because I felt an intense pain in my ankle, and my scar began to tingle.

Another voice was threatening to break through. I resisted as I held on for dear life to my necklace. I reached for Peter's hand. It was warm and soothing. Then I saw the fireflies and knew the voice would breakthrough, no matter how hard I tried to block the whispers. It seemed my newfound power would be tested again.

Don't miss out!

Visit the website below and you can sign up to receive emails whenever Victoria LK Williams publishes a new book. There's no charge and no obligation.

https://books2read.com/r/B-A-VGGF-QNDQ

BOOKS 2 READ

Connecting independent readers to independent writers.

Did you love *Whispered Voices*? Then you should read *Deceptive Voices*[1] by Victoria LK Williams!

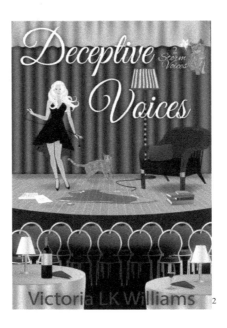

A flash of lightning is the warning of an approaching storm. But, for Mackenzie Aldkin, the lightning can signal something far more sinister.

With her newfound abilities to hear voices after a lightning strike, Mac is once again drawn into the planning of another murder. Or, so she thinks.

Set against the backdrop of a mystery theater production she is helping to put on, Mackenzie is finding it difficult to sort out what is real, and what is pretend.

With the help of her family and friends, along with her new kitten, Shaylee - who seems to have mystical powers of her own - it becomes a race against time for Mac to understand what the voices are telling her.

Can Mac trust what she hears long enough to prevent a murder? Or, are the voices possibly leading to her ominous end?

Read more at www.victorialkwilliams.com.

Also by Victoria LK Williams

Citrus Beach Mysteries
Murder for Neptune's Trident
Scent of a Mystery
Murder at the GeoCache
Runaway for Christmas
Tank Full of Trouble
The Flapper Caper
Borrowed, Blue, Dead
Trouble Has A Tail
Citrus Beach Mystery: Box Set: Books 1,2,3

Mrs. Avery's Adventures
Killer Focus
Final Delivery
The Dummy Did It

Sister Station Series
Now Arriving
Now Departing

Storm Voices
Whispered Voices
Deceptive Voices
Lost Voices

Tattle-Tale Mystery Novellas
The Toy Puzzle

Standalone
Cozy Christmas Collection

Watch for more at www.victorialkwilliams.com.

About the Author

Victoria believes that not everything can be answered by science. Faith and nature play a huge part in finding answers. Answers that often start with "what if".

*In her **Storm Voices** series, she wondered what would happen if you could hear the killers plans before they happen? And what if nature played a part in helping you solve the crime? With a love for gardening and watching lightning storms, the answers came to her enough to keep asking more questions and create a new series.*

*Currently, a new paranormal mystery series is in the draft stage: think murder, a ghost, and sea legends. Now start looking for the **Beach House Mystery Series**.*

Victoria also writes clean woman's fiction, with a touch of romance and a sprinkling of humor **Sister Station Series**. She also has two cozy Mystery Series **Citrus Beach Mysteries** and **Mrs. Avery's Adventures.**

She can often be found writing from her South Florida home, looking into her garden, watching the birds and squirrels fight over their next meal, while she writes. Her two cats, Miss Marple, and Fletch, often join her at the desk and each has their assigned spot. Victoria's not sure they are there to supervise her writing or watch the birds.

Victoria and her husband of 36 years share a love of gardening, and together they have written a gardening handbook for Florida gardeners.

Read more at www.victorialkwilliams.com.

About the Publisher

Books by our author, Victoria LK Williams have a tropical twist to them. Her characters are from the south, or are now in the south, but they all share a love of sun, sand & stories!

We are also pleased to offer the book **Pocket Guide to Florida Landscaping**, by *Donald R Williams*.

CPSIA information can be obtained
at www.ICGtesting.com
Printed in the USA
BVHW081550050321
601818BV00002B/535